I0571176

ONE KISS

WILD CANYON ESTATES STORIES, #4

TE SHERIDAN

One Kiss

by

TE Sheridan

Contemporary Romance Novella

Published by TE Sheridan

Edited by A. Marie

Cover Photo : Deposit Photos

Cover Design by Redbird Designs

All Rights Reserved

Copyright © 2020

ISBN#: 978-1-951637-08-8

Names, characters, and incidents depicted in this book are products of the author's imagination or are used fictitiously. Any resemblance to actual events, or person, living or dead, is coincidental and not the intent of the author.

No part of this book may be reproduced or transmitted in any form or by any means without permission in writing from the author.

Copyright © 2020 by TE Sheridan

All rights reserved.

No part of this book may be reproduced in any form or by any electronic or mechanical means, including information storage and retrieval systems, without written permission from the author, except for the use of brief quotations in a book review.

1

Legs spread wide, Konnor Horton tugged at the loose bindings on her wrists.

"Don't move." Evan Bellinger's voice was a sexy warning from the foot of the bed. She laughed softly and rolled her head on the mattress.

"How did I let you talk me into this?" She blinked under the blindfold and then licked her lips.

"I think in just a few minutes, you'll be very happy I talked you into this."

"Did you lock the door?" she asked again.

"I did."

"Maybe you should double check it."

"Already did," he reminded her. "Kon, relax. It's just me."

"I know." She whooshed out a deep breath. "I think it's the blindfold."

"Because you don't know where I'm gonna touch you."

"Yeah." She nodded. "I'm a little on edge."

"That's kind of the point."

She laughed again, but the feather light stroke of his fingers over the inside of her right ankle drew a sharp hiss.

"Fresh pedicure?" Evan pressed his thumb into her arch.

"Yes." The word escaped on a moan.

"It's very sexy."

"I'm lying here naked, spread out for your enjoyment, and you're admiring my pedicure?"

"You better believe I'm admiring every inch of your fuckable body right now, Konnor Horton."

She flinched at the use of her last name. Prayed he wouldn't notice, because now wasn't the time to get into how she wanted more from him and couldn't have it.

"You're not gonna pull out any whips and chains, are you?"

Evan's laugh chased a chill over her skin.

"Kon, you brought the sex toys," he reminded her. "I guess the question is do you have any whips and chains tucked away in that bag of yours."

"But you're the one who brought neckties and a blindfold."

"I'm not gonna hurt you."

Konnor gasped when he turned his attention to her other foot. He flicked the tip of his tongue over the center of her arch.

"Does this song ever end?" she mumbled as the thumping base of the techno beat outside the closed door pounded in her chest. The blindfold made this feel new and exciting, but Konnor would rather be alone with Evan at her apartment.

"Clearly, I need to speed things up if you're thinking about the music and not how I'm making you feel."

She smiled, but it was a weak attempt to put him off. Evan Bellinger made her feel all sorts of things that technically she shouldn't feel. Not since he had a wife somewhere at this party. True, she was most likely with someone else right now playing with her own sex toys. The party theme hadn't thrilled Konnor, but she had warmed to the idea. She had never been one to play on her own, because reaching orgasm had never been important to her. Not until she started this thing—whatever the hell you wanted to call it— with the Bellingers.

"Are you naked?" she asked him now. She wanted to want this. Her body wanted this. Seemed like her nipples had been hard for the last few days, anticipating the Wild Canyon Estates party. Her heart wanted this, wanted this night alone with Evan, while the rest of the world partied outside their locked door.

But her brain wanted to drag Konnor's ass up off the bed and back home. Alone. Her brain had a way of telling her things she didn't want to hear. Like how this was going nowhere. That it didn't matter if she was head over heels in love with Evan or Janie Bellinger, because they had each other, and she would never be first for either one of them.

"Not yet."

"Like? Nothing? You haven't taken anything off yet?"

"Why do you wanna know?"

Evan lifted her leg and set her foot on his shoulder. She felt his soft knit shirt under her skin.

"Because I can't see you." She rolled her lips inward and then sighed. "Are you still wearing your shoes?"

"The only clothing items I have removed tonight are from your body." He pressed his open mouth to the inside of her foot. "And by the way. The thong is in my pocket. And I'm not giving it back."

She laughed and then moaned softly when he stroked his hand down the back of her leg to mold his fingers over her ass cheek.

"Make sure you hide it before those pants go in the laundry." She gritted her teeth when he brushed his thumb over her seam, his thumb there and gone so quickly, she whimpered in protest.

"The boys don't do laundry," he promised her. "And Janie wears some pretty sexy stuff, too, so they wouldn't think twice, even if they did see it."

"Ev?"

"Hmm?"

"Don't do that, okay?"

"This?" He dragged the back of his knuckle over her clit. "Like touch you there? Or lick my finger?"

"Talk about Janie."

She struggled to blink away her emotion, grateful at the moment for the blindfold.

"Kon, Janie—"

"I know." She nodded and tugged at her hands again. Evan had bound her hands together over her head with a couple of neckties. They weren't tight, and she figured if she struggled hard enough, she could loosen the knots and be free. But part of her was incredibly turned on by the idea of Evan using her body any way he wanted for his entertainment, so she reminded herself to relax. "I know. You know how I feel about her."

"But?"

She bit her lip and then whooshed out another quick breath. No, this wasn't the time to tell him she was having second thoughts about their relationship. That as much as she loved them both, she couldn't keep up a threesome with a married couple. Her future looked a little lonely no matter how she looked at it. But with Evan and Janie in her life as they were, her loneliness was so much harder now knowing they were always together.

"Can tonight just be about us?"

The whispered words tore out of her mouth before she could stop them. At least she managed to shut her mouth before she said anymore.

"Anything you want, Konnor," he promised.

"I wanna blow your mind," she said simply. "I want you to think about me every time you bury your cock in your wife."

Behind the blindfold, she squeezed her eyes closed. Too far. She'd gone too far. Dammit, she knew better. They might need to talk, all three of them needed to talk, but Frank and Donna Jackson's house was not the place to say what she needed to say. And besides, on the off chance that this was her last night with Evan Bellinger, she wanted everything he could deliver.

Except his anger.

"Do you like being with her?" He spoke so quietly, Konnor couldn't tell if he was angry or not. "When it's just the two of you together?"

"Yes." Wasn't a lie. Konnor had slept with Janie as often as she had with Evan, and those nights had nothing to do with sleep and everything to do with sexual pleasure and gratification. And yes, Janie was one of her best friends.

But it had nothing to do with how she felt about Evan.

"She said she likes the way you kiss her better than I do."

Konnor held her breath for a second. "Your wife thinks I'm a better kisser than you are?"

"Apparently so."

"Did she specify what kind of kisses? Where?"

He laughed softly, and Konnor relaxed.

"No, but my point is that we all want to blow each other's minds, right?"

Maybe, but that wasn't what she wanted to say, what she wanted Evan to take from what she'd said.

"Just give me tonight," she whispered, serious again. "Please? Just you and me here together."

"Does your battery-operated boyfriend have a name?"

Konnor snorted and rolled her head back and forth on the bed.

"Are you cold?"

She gasped when his warm lips closed around her nipple.

"No, I'm just so fucking aroused, they've been like that for days."

"Why?" He scraped his teeth over the sensitive skin and closed them hard enough to make her yelp.

"Thinking about you."

"I think about you when I'm in the middle of meetings," he admitted. "I might be talking about cash flow statements or assets and liabilities, but my brain's picturing this, and my dick gets so hard, I feel like I could drill through a steel vault."

"Ev." She arched her back, desperate for him to touch her.

"Can you feel it now?" He stretched over her, his erection hard between her legs. "That's all for you, Konnor."

"I wanna touch you, Evan."

"Are you wet?"

"Maybe you should check your jeans." She nipped at his lips when he kissed her, but he· moved quickly to kiss her neck and then the pale, sensitive skin under her arm.

"You have sexy arms."

She chuckled and turned her head toward his.

"I want you inside me, Evan." She lifted her hips under his, but he straddled her to make her hold still.

"I promise you, I'm gonna get inside you, Kon. I can't wait to feel your pussy around my cock." He nipped at her inner elbow and then traced her skin with his tongue. "But I'm gonna take my time. And I'm gonna make you come first."

"Will you get naked?" She lifted her head from the bed to kiss the side of his face. "I wanna feel your skin on mine."

"Patience."

"I'm dying."

He scooted back over her body, his shirt soft on her breasts.

"You know, we could switch positions," she suggested. "I could tie you up and torture you."

"Do you have sex toys for me, too?" He grinned against her skin.

"Are you into anal beads?"

His face nuzzling her bare breasts, he stopped suddenly. Konnor could imagine him watching her.

"Please tell me you don't carry anal beads around with you."

"I don't carry around any sex toys with me," she answered simply. "The only reason I have what I do is because Janie strongly hinted that I might like them."

"Yeah? Do you guys use them? Like, do you use them on each other?"

"I don't wanna talk about Janie."

Evan laughed softly, but he dipped his head to suck the swell of her breast into his mouth again. With the blindfold on, she was lost in the sensation of his mouth on her breasts. He moved from one to the other, biting gently and sucking hard, making her moan and gasp with pleasure. The pressure of his fingers suddenly probing gently at her folds made her shiver.

"Not ready for that?" he teased her.

"Oh, god." She sobbed. "Please, Evan. I need you to touch me."

The bed moved under her, and she heard him moving, but she couldn't guess what he was doing. The song had finally changed out in the main part of the house, but to Konnor, the party playlist almost sounded like one super long song. She heard the rustle of clothing and hoped Evan was undressing, that he would forego the vibrator and drive into her with his cock.

"This looks interesting," he announced.

"What is it?"

"I'm gonna need…" The mattress gave when he knelt again. Konnor sighed with pleasure when his warm hands smoothed over her inner thighs. "Yep." He pressed her legs wide open. "Just like that."

"I don't think I could do this with anyone else," she whispered.

"Well, that's good to know."

She laughed sadly. Shouldn't it be okay for her to have this sort of intimacy, trust, with another man? With her *own* man?

"My stomach feels all fluttery," she admitted.

"You know I would never hurt you."

"I know." She nodded. "I don't think I've ever been blind-folded. It's just so bizarre, not knowing what you're going to do."

"I'm gonna make you feel like the only woman in the world," he told her. He teased her, wiggled his thumb over her clit and then lower.

"Yes."

She waited, assuming he would slide his fingers inside her and rub her clit with that thumb. When he didn't, she lifted her hips again in desperation. Instead of his fingers, it was his tongue she felt probe her gently.

"I can taste how bad you want this," he told her without lifting his face. His breath was warm on her wet, sensitive skin. "What's the longest word in the dictionary? Maybe I'll alphabet you."

"Evan," she whined.

"I love you," he said the words with his mouth pressed to her clit. The vibration made her shiver; his words made her eyes burn. You can't love me, she wanted to say. You can't love me enough, because you have to love her the most.

Evan swept his tongue up inside her, but she heard the sudden low hum of a battery-operated device.

"I'd rather just have you," she told him.

"I wanna watch you come." His voice was gruff. He pressed the suction end of her little vibrator to her clit and eased his fingers up inside her.

She laughed and sobbed at the same time. At the age of twenty-seven, at her friend and lover's direction, she had purchased two toys for her private pleasure. She'd put them both in the small bag she carried tonight. Neither failed to deliver on those nights when she was alone and needed company, something to keep her mind off of Evan fucking Janie. But the one Evan had chosen to play with was her favorite; she would come undone within minutes.

The thought of being bound and blindfolded with Evan watching her body writhe with pleasure took her breath away. But the truth that Evan knew she would prefer that particular toy because maybe his wife preferred her own— the same as Konnor's—to any other made Konnor a little sick to her stomach.

"It's on low," he told her. "Tell me if you want me to—"

She shook her head, the warm rush of pleasure already pulling at her.

"No. It's too fast."

"But it's more intense." His words were another reminder that Janie owned the same kind of toy and probably preferred it to any other. "Right?"

"Yes."

"Can you come more than once?" He swept the fingers buried inside her over the spot that would eventually make her weep with pleasure-pain. "With this?"

"Yes," she admitted. Evan changed the speed on the vibrator. Suddenly timid, Konnor wanted to shy away from the intimacy. Afraid of the intensity of the orgasm that was building, she tried to move, to close her legs.

"Don't."

The word was more of a plea than a command.

"Ev, I can't—"

"Come unglued for me, Konnor. Explode right here. It's me and you. Show me everything."

She moaned softly, hitched her hips when her thighs and her clit tingled with electric need.

"Evan."

"I've got you."

His promise drove her over the edge. Her voice broke on her scream, and she sobbed his name as her body—naked and vulnerable—quivered before him. Thankfully, he moved quickly, tossing her vibrator aside, sheathing his cock with a condom—Konnor heard the wrinkle of the plastic packaging —and driving into her with a possessive yank on her hips to pull her into him. She moved her hips with his as he pumped his cock in and out, and finally, desperate to put her arms around him, she yanked them free of the ties. Blood rushed through her forearms and hands as she wrapped them around Evan's back.

Konnor locked her ankles over his ass and moved with him, desperate for release again already.

"Kon?" Evan's voice was low and gritty next to her ear. Panting as she rocked her hips and clung to him, she only moaned in response. "Baby, I think of you every damned time I'm buried inside Janie's body."

2

The trouble with the Wild Canyon Estates parties was that she always went home alone. Worse than that, before the parties—before getting involved with the Bellingers—Konnor was happy on her own. She prided herself on her independence, but watching Evan and Janie together had taught her that independence didn't have to mean being alone. Lately, Konnor had been searching: her mind, and that was sure as hell a dark place to be, her heart, also dark. Her life. The trouble was she didn't know what she was searching for, only the disappointment that ate away at her when she didn't find it.

Evan used to insist on walking her up to the door of her second story, rooftop-entrance apartment. At first, she had been so charmed by that, by him, that she'd thought it was sweet. Not to mention that it allowed them a few extra kisses before the night was over. But the charm had worn off, and by the end of that ride home on the nights Evan drove, she was desperate to walk away from her friends and be alone.

For the better part of a year now, she had been working to free herself from her stepbrothers' power over her. Not to make it sound dramatic; Ryan and Luke didn't have anything to blackmail her with. They wouldn't do that to her anyway. But she had always adored them both, even when they were kids, which was how she'd ended up living the life she was living. She had announced last year around the holiday season that she didn't want to do it anymore. She didn't want to entertain her stepbrothers' friends or colleagues. No amount of cash would change her mind; she was ready to put that part of her life behind her.

They argued with her. Tried to sweet talk her into coming back for their cocktail parties that involved a lot more than cocktails. She had made the drive occasionally over the past several months, but she had also flat out refused on more than one occasion. She didn't love the things she'd done in her past, though she made no apologies for who she was. But she was determined to end her business agreement with Ryan and Luke. Hard to draw that line, though, as was sometimes the case with mixing family and business.

But any pride she had in finding her backbone where her stepbrothers were concerned kind of vanished when she spent too much time thinking about her latest colossal mistake. Sure, she loved Janie and Evan. They treated her like family. She was crazy about their sons; Andrew and Gavin knew her as a close family friend. But she would never have Evan or Janie completely and totally to herself, and any time she spent with either of them had to be a secret.

It wasn't that long ago that it wouldn't have mattered to her. She had understood her place, her path in life, before she was twenty years old. Love was doubtful. Marriage, kids, picket fences—not for her. But then she'd gone and fallen for someone, and he had the marriage *and* the kids *and* the picket fences.

She told him that sometimes. When they were alone at

the Jacksons' parties, cuddled up together on a lounge chair, both fully clothed and just enjoying each other's company. When they were alone in one of the Jacksons' bedrooms, door closed and locked, and Evan was buried as deep inside her as he could get, those words would slip out. The first time she'd said it with no qualifying words added to it, the first time she'd just gushed *I love you* as he moved inside her, their eyes had met in the dimly lit room. Evan had kissed her; she loved the way he kissed her. He might have said something in return, but when he ended the kiss and looked at her again, she simply shook her head.

He couldn't love her. Not like that. Not when he was married. Not when he was married to her good friend. But Konnor had given up trying to hide what she felt for him. And Janie. She decided to let him say the words back to her, because odds were, she'd never hear another man tell her he loved her.

Some mornings after the Wild Canyon parties, Evan and Janie showed up with coffee or breakfast. There were times when Konnor wasn't in the mood for a visit, but she always welcomed them with a smile. Those mornings were calm and quiet; in Konnor's mind, those visits were more like friends hanging out and spending time together than lovers flirting or letting sexual tension build again.

Konnor climbed out of bed and used the bathroom, careful not to look too closely at herself in the mirror over the sink. Her reflection wasn't bad, but mornings were rough, and mornings after those parties tended to be a little bit harder to face herself. She padded barefoot to the kitchen, hands cupping her face and then shoving her hair back out of her eyes. She shot a glance at her small dinette set and frowned when she saw her backpack where she'd left it last night after class. Homework. As soon as Evan and Janie left, she would have to tackle her accounting assignment.

With a yawn, she walked through the motions of making coffee and then stood with her back against the counter and her feet stacked one on top of the other and thought about the party last night. She'd been involved with the Bellingers for a few months. She and Evan and Janie had done every dirty thing together she could dream of, but something about the blindfold and Evan watching her while he pleasured her last night had ripped away her sense of security. Even after they made love, when they curled up together in their little slice of privacy, she had felt raw and exposed, and right about now, her stomach twisted with regret.

The light tap on her door stirred her into action. Her apartment occupied the entire second floor of a big brick bungalow in Rockfield's historic district. It unnerved her when someone showed up unannounced and headed up the back stairs to knock like that. Even Evan and Janie. Even when she knew they would probably show up.

Still in a skimpy pair of athletic shorts and the oversized sweatshirt she'd pulled on when she climbed out of bed, she rubbed her eyes as she slipped out the kitchen doorway and unlocked her door.

"Hey—" She stopped talking when she realized it wasn't Evan and Janie at the door. Caught off guard, she hunched her shoulders and crossed her arms over her chest. She caught herself before she could step backward. Konnor refused to cower, to show any weakness.

"Hey." His voice was low and gruff now, reminding her that he hadn't been much older than the Bellinger boys the last time she saw him. With her heart in her throat, Konnor struggled to maintain eye contact with him. Fall colors in the trees surrounding the house offered a tempting distraction, but she held her head high and stared at him boldly.

"Blaize."

"Busy?"

She bit her lip and nodded. What the hell was Blaize Stewart doing in her town, at her apartment, right at this instant? She hadn't seen him in at least six years. She hadn't *talked* to him in at least six years, maybe longer.

"I am." She nodded again. "What're you doing here?"

"In town for a few days on business," he answered vaguely. "Luke mentioned that you were living here."

Konnor eyed Blaize suspiciously for a second and then laughed softly, the sound heavy with sarcasm.

"What do you want?"

"Nothing." Blaize held his hands up apologetically. "I just thought we could hang out. Reminisce."

"What do you do?"

"What?"

"For work. You said you're in town on business," she reminded him. "What do you do?"

"I'm a civil engineer."

"And you're here? Working in Rockfield?"

"Possibly consulting on the new clinic project," he said simply. The city was looking to throw the coffers into a new building for a women's center. The space would include the required exam rooms, offices, ultrasound equipment, a daycare facility, an outpatient surgery center, a coffee shop, and a parking deck. Konnor wasn't sure how anyone thought they were going to fit all of that in the allocated spot, but then she wasn't a civil engineer or the city manager or mayor, and she had no idea where she would settle down when she was done with school. So, no, she didn't care much about it.

Deflated, Konnor rolled her eyes and stepped back. She didn't want him here; she would have been happy if she never saw Blaize Stewart again in her life. But she wasn't rude. She couldn't just slam the door in his face.

"Do you wanna come in?"

Blaize hesitated at her flat, emotionless invitation. If it was warmer, she would invite him to sit at the patio table on the rooftop. But she was chilled, and she preferred to wrap up their reminiscing before the Bellingers showed up. She had no desire to make introductions.

"I'm cold." She shrugged. "Stay or go. I don't care."

She turned her back to him and moved back to the kitchen, leaving the door open. When she heard him step inside and close the door, she let out the pent-up breath she hadn't realized she was holding. She wanted him to leave. Right? Konnor had nothing to say to Blaize Stewart, and she wasn't interested in anything he had to say, so catching up would be a waste of time.

"Luke gave you my address?" she asked without looking at him.

"No."

The sound of his voice in her apartment was surreal after all the years that had passed with no contact. Konnor glanced at him over her shoulder. His wide shoulders took up the kitchen doorway, but somehow his presence—the fact that he was here, in her apartment where she lived and breathed and slept—filled the whole room around her.

"Then what did you mean?"

"He mentioned a while back that you were living in Rockfield." Blaize shrugged. "I looked you up."

"Why?" she asked him. "Why would you bother to look me up now? After all these years?"

"I told you. I thought it would be fun to hang out again."

Konnor sighed, but she turned her head when she heard her phone buzzing. She mumbled to him to excuse her and unzipped her bag to dig her phone out. She hadn't charged it the night before, but she still had some battery life left.

"Hey." She answered Janie's call with her back to Blaize. "What's up?"

"Do you want blueberry scones or muffins?"

Not in the mood for her friend's exuberance today, not in the mood for choices, not in the mood for her friends at all now, Konnor clamped her mouth closed on a frustrated sigh.

"You pick."

"Ev wants muffins."

"Then get muffins," Konnor said quietly. "That's fine."

"Need us to get coffee?"

"No. I made some."

"Okay. See you in a few."

Konnor ended the call and then folded her arms over her chest again, tucking the phone at her side.

"Do I need to go? Or do I get some of that coffee?"

Startled by the sound of his voice again and by his request for coffee, which would mean he would most likely still be here when Evan and Janie arrived, Konnor cleared her throat and turned to look at him. He was closer now, standing just behind her. Hands tucked in his hip pockets, he looked harmless.

For Konnor, Blaize Stewart was anything but harmless.

"If I give you coffee, will you leave?"

"I'm not asking for a travel mug, Konnor. I want to talk to you."

Konnor drew a deep breath and dropped her arms to her sides. She set her phone on the counter again and ran her fingers through her hair.

"Fine." She shook her head and shrugged at the same time. He stepped out of her way, but she felt his gaze on her as she took four mugs from the cabinet above the coffee maker. "Do you talk to Luke a lot?"

The idea of Blaize keeping in touch with either of her stepbrothers bothered her, but she didn't want to admit it.

"No. Not at all, really." He stepped up beside her as she poured coffee into two of the mugs. "I was back home in

January. My sister had a baby. Ran into Luke at the grocery store when I went on a coffee run for Mom."

His words hurt, though it was unintentional. Mandi Stewart had a kid. Konnor didn't even want kids, but she wanted the right to have them, the love to make them, if she changed her mind.

"And what? He just announced that I was living in Rockfield?"

"No."

She pushed a mug his way over the counter, careful not to slosh hot coffee over the rim. Her phone buzzed and a text from Evan popped up on the screen. Thankfully, it was only a picture of the display of goodies at the Bellingers' favorite bakery.

"Evan." Blaize read the name. "So, you're dating someone?"

"How did it come up? That I was living in Rockfield?" Konnor ignored his question and answered with one of her own.

"I told him I was looking at moving here. That I was in meetings with the city planner about the clinic project. He told me to look you up."

Konnor was torn between wanting to thank Luke—more like give him hell—for sending Blaize back into her life and wondering why it had taken Blaize all of spring and summer to look her up if he had known where to find her.

"He said you went back to school."

"I did." She nodded.

"That's great."

"Don't patronize me, Blaize." Her whisper was gruff. "You don't know me. Not anymore."

Technically, she wasn't sure Blaize had ever really known her, though they had been thick as thieves when they were kids.

"Why are you so touchy?"

Rather than look him in the eyes, Konnor stared at his hand, his long fingers wrapped around the chunky mug. He made the oversized mug look small. Konnor remembered a time when all she wanted was his hands on her, his arms around her.

"Is he on the way over here? Your boyfriend?"

"He's not—" She stopped talking. What was the point in trying to explain to him who Evan was to her? Good grief, most of the time, she wasn't sure what Evan was to her. How the hell could she make Blaize understand the relationship she had with a married man and his wife? And more importantly, why should she explain anything to him?

"What're you studying?" He changed tactics. When he lifted the mug to drink from it, Konnor lifted her gaze to watch him.

"I'm majoring in business," she answered.

"Good for you."

She tipped her head, eyebrows at her hairline.

"I'm not patronizing you." He rolled his eyes. "I'm glad you're doing something with your life."

"And here we go," she mumbled. She picked up her own mug and wandered over to the table. "Fire away."

She moved her backpack to the floor and lowered herself to sit on her bent leg.

"How often do you see Luke and Ryan?" Leaning on the counter facing her, he folded his arms over his chest. Konnor wondered if he was asking if she visited as part of the family or if he knew about her side occupation the past several years. Odds were, he had known at some point that she was still entertaining her stepbrothers' friends, just on a higher scale. Higher-class sex. She got to wear sexy dresses and stilettos, and the pay scale was a hell of a lot better now.

"Not often." She kept her answer purposefully vague.

"Well, I'm sure you have plenty here to keep you busy." He sounded conversational now. Konnor watched him push off the counter and reach for the mug again. His eyes swept over her bag and the stovetop and finally, he looked at her again. "But I'll be spending a lot of time here for a while. I was hoping we could reconnect."

"Re—? Reconnect?" She coughed. They'd never connected in the first place. At least not the way she wanted to all those years ago.

"Nachos and beer. A movie. Miniature golf."

She waited to see if he threw in playing Pig or fucking around, surprised when he turned hopeful eyes to her.

"I don't think so, Blaize." She shook her head.

"Why not?"

She jumped when the loud knock on her door banged through the room.

"Because of him?"

"No." She shrugged as she climbed to her feet. "Because of me. And you."

"What does that mean?" he called after her as she slipped from the room to get the door. "We were friends, K."

"Hey." She pulled the door open and offered her friends a lame, tired smile.

"Hey." When Janie stepped inside first, Konnor noticed she and Evan were holding hands. "How are you this morning?" Sweeping in close, Janie cupped the back of Konnor's neck in her free hand and kissed the corner of her mouth. "You look tired."

Konnor met Evan's eyes but said nothing when he gave her a lopsided grin.

"Yeah," Konnor lied. "I guess I am. Come in."

Butterflies raged in her belly as she led Janie and Evan into the kitchen. This was a scene she had never dreamt would unfold; one she certainly didn't want to deal with.

Never mind that she and Blaize had never been intimately involved. She saw the way Evan puffed up his chest with that ridiculous male bravado the second he laid eyes on Blaize. Evan wouldn't believe a word she said to him. Not after finding Blaize in her apartment, when she was still wearing what she'd slept in.

"Hey." Janie pretended to be oblivious to the tension in the room.

Konnor cleared her throat. "Janie, Evan, this is Blaize Stewart. Blaize and I knew each other when we were kids." She skated her gaze over all three of them, cataloguing the curiosity, the suspicion, and the disgust on each of their faces. "Blaize, my friends Janie and Evan Bellinger."

"It's nice to meet you." Blaize recovered first, wiping that look of disgust, of horror, from his face and reaching to shake Janie's hand. He flashed her a charming smile. Konnor turned away, reminded again that he had never wanted her, loved her, the way she had him.

She poured coffee for Janie and Evan and then took saucers from the cabinet, but the actions—the pretending that everything was normal about this mix of people in her kitchen—made her tense. Fear of what might be said pounded a headache between her eyes.

"Did you go to school with Konnor?" Janie's chirpy voice grated on Konnor's last nerve. Hostess duties fulfilled, Konnor skipped a muffin of her own, and crossed the room to sit again at the table. She let her eyes roam the room, watched the way Janie's hungry eyes devoured Blaize. When Konnor had known him years ago, he'd had a baby face. The guys had always ribbed him, because he had a hard time growing facial hair. Konnor remembered thinking he looked sweet, which made his indifference to her affection that much harder to take. He was an athlete back in their school days; he had played baseball and basketball. She'd watched him and all the other guys play at home games, and she'd been all in, jumping into any car heading to away games, ready to hang with the crowd.

Turning her attention from Janie, past the scowl on Evan's face, Konnor eyed Blaize now. He was wearing long-sleeves, but it looked like he might still work out. His shoulders were wide, and his thighs filled his worn denim. Konnor had no doubt his ass probably looked just as good, but she wasn't going to ask him to pirouette for her.

His face was harder now. A little bit angular, with strong cheekbones and a sharp nose. His cool blue eyes framed in thick, long lashes would make any woman weep. She was drawn to the scruff on his face and his unruly, dirty-blond hair, curled around his ears and his collar. A shock of it fell over his forehead and gave him a sexy, bad boy look. Maybe what he wanted to accomplish all those years ago but couldn't.

"Yeah." Blaize shrugged and nodded his head back and forth. "I knew Konnor in school. I'm from Averill. Grew up with Konnor and her stepbrothers."

"Really?" Evan nodded. He sounded deceptively calm, but Konnor noticed the squaring of his shoulders and the firm set of his jaw. He had made no secret of how he felt about her stepbrothers and her introduction to sex. Now he thought he had a target for his anger.

Konnor silently wished that Blaize would finish his coffee quickly and go. The less conversation between him and the Bellingers, the better.

"K and I used to spend a lot of time together." The sad smile on his face when he jerked his head in her direction zapped her in the heart. They had spent a lot of time together, time during which she was pining away for him and he was either clueless or flat out not interested.

"Yeah? And that was—"

"Why don't you guys sit down?" Konnor interrupted Evan. "Grab a muffin."

Janie must have sensed Konnor's discomfort. She patted Evan's arm and steered him back to the counter. Blaize, however, kept his eyes on Konnor as he stepped toward her to set his cup on the table.

"Good to see you, Konnor." His comment was lukewarm, definitely not convincing. "I'll get out of your way."

She watched, stunned, as he slipped out the doorway.

"Blaize?" she called softly, and then louder again, as she scrambled off her chair to follow him out of the kitchen and out the door onto the rooftop. "You're—? You show up out of nowhere and say three words, and now you're just walking out?"

"You're busy." He shrugged his lips, distaste written all over his face. "I get it."

"What?"

"I saw her kiss you when they came in," he told her. "And I noticed your sex toys in your bag when you answered the door. No wonder you don't have time to work for Luke and Ryan anymore."

Konnor opened her mouth to speak, but when she found no words, she clamped her teeth together hard enough to hurt and crossed her arms over her chest.

"Little sister's movin' up in the world." He tipped his head and raised his eyebrows. "I'd ask you to dinner tonight, but I don't wanna be penciled in in between jobs."

"Blaize." She sank her teeth into her lower lip. When he turned to walk away, Konnor almost reached out for him. She dropped her arms but caught herself before she could move close enough to actually touch him. Instead, she watched him disappear around the side of the rooftop, down the side stairs.

Her eyes filled with tears she didn't want to cry. Crying

made her feel weak, and she didn't do it often. But Blaize Stewart had always had that power over her; he'd made her cry more than once when they were younger.

"Kon?"

She lifted her chin when she heard Janie open the door behind her.

"I'm coming," she whispered, certain Janie didn't hear her. Needing a moment to pull herself together, she dabbed at her eyes and concentrated on swallowing the knife in her throat.

3

Sometimes, the morning-after coffee visits were fun: talking, kissing, smoking-hot make out sessions, even just sitting on the rooftop and listening to the breeze rustle the leaves. This wasn't going to be fun. Not now, not after Blaize had shown up, and not after Evan and Janie had seen him here.

They would demand answers Konnor didn't want to give. First of all, she had told Evan when she'd gone to her first party at Wild Canyon Estates that she didn't want to go into personal stuff. And then she'd gone down on him and had sex with him while his wife watched, and things had gone to hell from there.

Well, not really. Konnor had run from them, but in the end, they'd drawn her backstory from her and loved her anyway. But she didn't want to tell them *this* part of the story. It was humiliating, and it was the one part of the whole sordid tale that hurt, and she sure as hell didn't want to invite that heartache back in.

Still. She couldn't stand out here forever just to avoid them. Her feet were so cold, her toes were going numb. And the longer she left Evan and Janie inside, alone, the longer the questions would fester, the harder to put Evan's anger at ease.

She heard the door close again, and she drew in a deep breath, hoping she was inhaling courage. But as she turned back to the door, a flash of movement and color at the side of the rooftop caught her attention.

"Blaize?"

He stood at the top of the steps, hands propped on his hips and head cocked.

"What?" A flurry of emotions sucked her courage and her voice away and left her weak in the knees. "What do you want?"

He stalked across the rooftop until he stood so close to her, she could feel the brush of his denim on her bare legs. He blocked the wind, but her body still shivered with the cold and fear.

"Did you leave something in the house?"

He answered her whisper with a shake of his head and lifted his hand to play with the ends of her hair.

"One kiss." He slid the pad of his finger over the hardware in her ear, drawing a deep shiver up her spine. Evan liked to kiss her there.

"What?"

Blaize shook his head, and then that finger was on her lips. His heated gaze was bold and unforgiving as he studied her face, her parted lips, but he didn't look away. She should stop him. Ask him to leave.

Not because of Janie or Evan.

Because when she wanted this all those years ago, Blaize had looked at her with a blank face and taken both of her hands in one of his and gently pushed her away.

She didn't want to stop him. She didn't want to ask him to leave.

One kiss.

She wanted this one kiss before he disappeared from her life again.

His fingers fanned her face, and he leaned closer to kiss her. Konnor kept her eyes open, desperate to memorize the moment. The look on his face. His lashes on his cheek when he closed his eyes. The pale pink skin of his lips just before he pressed them to hers. He settled his free hand at her side. No groping. No trying to push her top up to paw at her skin.

He smelled clean and masculine. His light scent filled her, and then he rubbed his lips over hers. Gentle. Curious. Scared he would walk away too soon, Konnor held herself completely still, afraid to even kiss him back. She angled her head slowly, hoping he would see it as an offering and not an attempt to take control.

She shivered again, goosebumps climbed her bare legs and traced her upper body, under the sweatshirt, when he swept his warm, wet tongue over her lips. She wanted to touch him, to touch the scruff on his face. She wanted to kiss him back. Just to touch his tongue with hers, to explore the taste and texture of his mouth.

Blaize rubbed the center of her upper lip with the tip of his tongue and then drew back, as if waiting for her to respond. Finally, Konnor squeezed her eyes closed. To hide her tears. Still afraid he would walk away, she parted her lips further and waited.

When he kissed her again, she kissed him back. Still careful, still more tender than bold and sexual. Because this was her last chance, she lifted her hands. Rested them on his upper arms. Fingers restless, still craving the feel of his scruff, she rubbed light circles on his shirt, wishing she could be brave. Wishing she could kiss him like she wanted to. Knowing she would only be affirming what he thought of her.

But, still, he kissed her. Soft and sweet and deeply, he kissed her. Konnor's hands moved without her permission. She curled her fingers into fists, reminded herself that he didn't want her. Not like this. He never had. He didn't want her hands on him. Not even on his face.

He pulled back when she touched him. Just a featherlight stroke of her fingertips over the scruff on his cheek. Konnor sobbed softly as she blinked her eyes open. His electric blue eyes were so much closer than they'd ever been, but she couldn't read his thoughts. She couldn't see his soul, but then he would never give her that. She knew that. One kiss might satisfy his curiosity, but it wasn't going to ignite some crazy, passionate love affair.

Without a word, he took her hands in his and pushed her away gently. Konnor sniffled and swiped at her eyes as he backed away and turned to the steps.

"Blaize." She spoke softly.

He stopped at the steps, but he didn't look at her. Konnor watched his shoulders tense, like he thought she might throw herself at him and cause a scene.

"Do I owe you for that?" He threw her a cool look over his shoulder.

When their eyes met, Konnor dipped her chin to her chest, ashamed of the memories between them. Unwilling to let him have the last word, to let him speak to her that way, she took a deep breath and swallowed more courage.

"Don't come back." Her voice was cold and hard as steel.

She waited until she was sure he was gone before turning to join Evan and Janie inside. Tempted to walk right past the kitchen and hide in the bathroom for a few minutes, Konnor hesitated when Janie shot out of her chair and hurried to the coffee maker to refill Konnor's mug. She couldn't hide that she was upset. She could sit here with them and let them see her tears, or she could lock herself in the bathroom to wash her face, in which case they would know exactly what she was doing anyway.

"You okay?" Janie met her in the doorway. No kiss this time. Just her friend's arms around her, holding her for a second. Konnor gave herself a few seconds before she forced herself to nod and gently push Janie away.

"Why was he here?" Evan, standing at the counter, moved closer to Konnor when Janie returned to the table to sit. He leaned in close enough to brush his lips over Konnor's cheek and her ear. The touch was suggestive of the way he often played with the studs and hoops in the shell of her ear, most often when she had her mouth on his cock.

"Long story." Konnor joined Janie at the table.

"Did he rape you? When you were younger?"

"No."

Evan carried the bakery box to the table and eyed her suspiciously.

"Don't argue semantics with me, Kon. Did that guy fuck you? Make you—"

"No." She shook her head, praying that Evan would let it go. The fact that Blaize had never been interested in touching her was more humiliating to her than if he had fucked her.

"Why was he here?"

"I don't know, Evan." She covered her face with her hands and forced the words out with a frustrated sigh. She wished she could start the morning over, so she could at least be prepared for this conversation. Better yet, she wished Blaize wouldn't have just shown up here unannounced. That he wouldn't have rubbed elbows with the Bellingers.

That he wouldn't have finally decided to claim one kiss.

She had to tell Janie and Evan the truth. It wasn't right to let Evan assume the worst about Blaize, and neither of them would be angry with her for the truth. She just didn't relish the thought of climbing back into the past. She didn't exactly regret the things she'd done with Luke and Ryan and their friends. Up until this summer, she had been so focused on her future, the past didn't matter at all.

But guys like Blaize Stewart made her regret things. Guys like Blaize Stewart showing up and thinking the worst of her and then kissing her anyway and walking away made her regret a lot of things.

Why had she let him kiss her?

Why had she let his kiss get to her, just as she had known it would?

"Did you sleep with him?" Janie asked softly.

Konnor lowered her hands slowly and looked first at Janie and then Evan.

"What?"

"You have a past with him," Janie offered. Konnor wondered if that was an excuse for why Janie had asked or if she thought she'd given Konnor a way out, an excuse for sleeping with someone else.

"I was with you guys last night," Konnor reminded them.

"You were home at midnight."

"And you think after what we did, I came home and found him on the steps and invited him in?" Konnor turned to Evan with a frown.

"Because." Janie shrugged and rubbed her fingertips over her mouth. She tipped her head to study Konnor, obviously wanting to say more but worried she would overstep. "I mean…"

"He showed up here about ten minutes before you did."

"I get it," Janie continued, as if Konnor hadn't spoken. "He's your age. He's single. He's…" She stopped talking, wagged her eyebrows, and laughed. The soft sound hit Konnor like a bullet. "Pretty easy on the eyes."

Blaize Stewart was so easy on the eyes, it hurt to look at him. But Konnor didn't comment.

"But." Janie glanced at Evan. "I don't know, Kon. This is…hard."

Konnor stared at Janie silently for a moment. It intrigued her that Janie could approach her as a girlfriend and say the right things about Blaize being easy on the eyes which apparently would make it acceptable if Konnor had slept with him. But that Evan—her husband—was upset that Konnor might have slept with someone from her past.

Janie appeared to be as concerned for Evan as she was for Konnor.

Konnor wondered now what Evan would say if she found someone to love her the way he loved Janie. Would he let her go? Without a fight?

"I haven't been with anyone but you guys since that first night we were together." She cleared her throat. "And I've never slept with Blaize."

When Janie didn't say anything, Konnor glanced at Evan. He huffed out a sigh and sank down at the table across from her.

"You don't believe me." She swallowed hard and took a deep breath. Janie pulled the bakery box closer, but Konnor only stared at it and then Janie. "Of course, you don't believe me. Hazard of the side job, right?"

"It's not even what you did or didn't do with him." Evan sounded tired. He tapped his fingers on the tabletop. "It's why he was here. And why you spent any time with him at all."

"Ev." Janie touched the back of his hand.

Eyes on the box, Konnor bristled at Janie's tone. The way she was placating Evan. Warning him to take it easy on Konnor. She didn't take kindly to a man demanding answers from her. Not a married man who enjoyed her company in his bed. There was more to it, yes. Evan and Janie felt something for her, though, probably not at the same level she was feeling things for them.

"I did not invite him here, if that's what you're implying." She finally lifted her gaze from the box and stared Evan down.

"And yet, he was here, and you obviously just got out of bed."

Konnor reminded herself that they were sort of in a relationship. Evan had the right to know if she slept with someone else. Right? He knew she used to go home on occasion to help Ryan and Luke out, even though she had told her stepbrothers she didn't want to anymore. She hadn't gone home since she'd been involved with the Bellingers. But if they were lovers, did he have the right to know if she was with someone else? If Blaize had stayed last night, would she tell Evan and Janie?

That emptiness inside her yawned a little bigger at the thought. If Blaize had stayed...

Evan stared at her expectantly when she shook herself out of that daydream.

"I got home close to midnight and went to bed. Got up this morning, started making coffee, and heard the knock on the door. I assumed it was you guys." Konnor licked her lips. "It was Blaize. That's it."

Evan leaned forward and rested his elbows on the table. Konnor watched him rub his eyes and then scrub his fingers back over his head.

"I just...whatever you're doing now...the men you're with..." He sighed. "I don't know. I'm picturing it similar to Frank and Donna's parties. Maybe a bit more discreet, classier. And not the frat boy vibe I get from when you were younger."

"Evan." Her voice broke, but she took a deep breath, wincing at the pain, and steeled herself.

"I don't get why you sell yourself, Konnor, but I really don't get why you would invite that sort of thing back into your life now."

She whooshed out a slow, sad sigh and rubbed her eyes. She'd never told Evan and Janie that entertaining her stepbrothers' friends was like being entertainment at a frat party. Probably, it was. But when she was in the thick of it, she hadn't cared. Again—validation to Konnor that she knew what she was doing and that she had been in charge.

"What part of that am I supposed to answer?" Konnor finally asked him. She circled her hands around her coffee mug and flicked her gaze to Janie as she served each of them a muffin. Normally, Konnor would dive in and wolf the muffin down. Right now, her stomach recoiled at the thought of eating.

"Whatever you're comfortable sharing, I guess." Evan shrugged.

She hated that slack look on his face. Considered climbing over the table to smack it off him. A tiny part of her liked that he wanted to protect her, that he seemed jealous of the things she'd done with clients at the parties she attended. That he was suspicious and jealous of what might have happened with Blaize. And yet, she considered reminding him that he was married, and he had no right to feel any of that, because she didn't really belong to him. Not to mention, there were nights Evan and Janie were intimate without her. The wedding rings were a big reminder of that, but it was still hard to swallow sometimes.

"The parties now are more like the Wild Canyon parties," she said quietly. "It's not a big orgy with everyone walking around topless or nude. It's very classy, actually. Luke and Ryan are big businessmen, and they run a first-class show. I didn't have sex with the majority of the people…that hired me."

"So, you were there to put your mouth on their dicks and suck 'em off. And then you collected your money and went home."

Konnor flinched. Evan's frosty tone reminded her too much of the scene with Blaize a few minutes ago on the rooftop.

"You don't mind it when I suck you off, Evan," she reminded him.

"That's different," he argued.

She nodded, because it was different.

Sort of.

But the wedding band on his finger sort of made it the same.

"As for the stuff when I was younger, yeah, it was…" She licked her lips and closed her eyes. Rested her elbows on the table and covered her face with her hands. "It was a free for all, and it was okay. I've told you over and over, it's all okay. They didn't hurt me. None of them hurt me. They were like extra big brothers. They took care of me."

"The Konnor Horton I know is a proud, independent woman who doesn't need to be taken care of."

"I had to grow into that woman, Evan."

"So. This guy." Evan leaned back in his chair and crossed his arms over his chest. "He never hurt you."

She lowered her hands to the table and sniffled.

"He did." She shrugged. "Blaize hurt me. And he did it again just now, but I promise you he won't be back."

"Where is he?" Evan stood so quickly, the red vinyl covered chair tipped over and crashed to the floor.

"I have no idea where he is, but it's not like that," she whispered. "I've never slept with Blaize Stewart. I've never touched him. Never…" She peeked at Evan and shook her head.

"Then what's the story, Kon? I wanted to break his face when I walked in and found him here with you. And then you introduced him as someone from your past, and I wanted to pound his teeth down his throat."

Konnor smiled and glanced at Janie.

"Kon, we love you," Janie said quietly. "This guy—"

"Blaize was never into me," Konnor interrupted Janie, because she needed this conversation to be over. She'd already given Blaize way too damned much of her time. Time to sweep it up and away. She also had no desire to delve into the conversation that the three of them should probably have in the near future. How the hell had they gone from a steamy threesome at a party to being involved in an intimate, emotional affair that had nowhere to go?

Then again, maybe for Evan and Janie, that was okay. They were at a different place in their lives. Careers. Marriage. Children. Konnor knew that was out of the question for her, but still, how long could she be in love with a married couple? Maybe she wasn't cut out for marriage and children, but didn't she deserve a shot at an exclusive relationship of her own?

"We were friends." Konnor rubbed her eyes and then flipped her hair back from her face. "I don't think you guys get that. Until that summer, I was just one of the guys. We were all friends. We did everything together. And then we threw in some experimenting. It wasn't like gang rape. It was more like… Ry and Luke had a few guys over, and they played video games, and maybe one of them undressed me and we fooled around."

"While the rest of them watched."

"Sometimes," Konnor admitted. "But not Blaize. As far as I know, he never looked at me. Ever. Now and then, one of the guys would razz him about being gay if he didn't want to touch me."

"And that's how he hurt you?" Janie fiddled with her muffin, though none of them had taken a bite yet.

"I liked him," Konnor admitted. "You said something that night at your house, when I tried to walk away. About losing my first kiss to something...bad."

"Konnor, I don't think you're bad—"

Konnor shook her head and held her hand up to stop Janie. "Blaize was my first crush. I loved him fiercely, like only a thirteen-year-old girl can madly love a boy. I drew hearts with his initials in them. I wrote my name with his last name. I daydreamed about holding his hand at school, about kissing him."

"Ohhh." Janie nodded. "I get it."

Konnor raised her eyebrows and forced herself to go on.

"He didn't. He didn't get it. At fifteen, he was into baseball and bikes and video games. Boy stuff. We spent a lot of time together. We rode our bikes everywhere, and he and I played Pig every day unless it was raining. I had a great shot, but he was just a little bit better than me. We laughed together. We had fun."

"What happened?" Evan's voice was gruff.

"He never got the message, I guess. That I liked him as more than a friend. And he asked someone else to go to homecoming with him when he was a sophomore. I was crushed, but I was determined that one day he would notice me. When the rest of the boys did, when we started fooling around, I thought finally Blaize would want to kiss me."

"He didn't."

"No." She shook her head. "There was one night when he was leaving. I had been upstairs in my room. Nothing happened that night. The guys were watching movies. Horror movies, I think? And I came downstairs to get a snack as Blaize was leaving. It was just the two of us in the kitchen, and he stood at the counter…close enough to me for me to think maybe he finally *saw* me. But when I moved closer, he changed. It was like he put a mask on. Cold. Indifferent. I tried to touch him, to put my hands on his face. He pushed my hands away and walked out with a mumbled goodbye, and that was that."

"You never talked to him again?"

"Yeah, but we never had a moment. Never had that window of opportunity. I think he made sure of that. The last time I saw him before this morning was maybe six years ago. We were at a local fall festival. All of us. I was in the econ class at the time, and I was sort of seeing the professor, but nothing serious had happened yet. Blaize said he had a girlfriend at school, and it crushed me, and when I left the park that night, I tucked him away and didn't look back."

"But he showed up this morning. Here. Out of the blue."

She nodded. "He's a civil engineer, and he's consulting on the clinic project. Said he knew I lived here. Still talks to my stepbrothers occasionally but hasn't seen them in years."

"He hurt you? Before we got here? Outside?" Evan prompted her. "Did he put his hands on you?"

"No, Evan." Konnor shook her head. "He didn't. He said something that dragged all of this back up. Made me remember that crush. The way I moped over him when I was a stupid girl who thought I could have something…like you guys do."

4

Lies of omission were as heavy as real untruths spoken aloud. Five days after telling Evan and Janie that Blaize hadn't touched her the morning after the Wild Canyon Estates party, Konnor still had indigestion from swallowing the words about the kiss. She wasn't sure why she hadn't just told them. It wasn't as if the kiss meant anything anyway. She wouldn't see Blaize again; he wasn't walking around with his head in the clouds thinking about her.

She was thinking about him, though. Which made her angry. With him. With herself. With the world.

Konnor worked her part time hours at the bank, dodged a call from Ryan, took another call from Ryan, and argued that she wouldn't just drive home Wednesday evening for his cocktail party. Most of her classes this semester were in the late afternoon and evening hours, and she had no intention of missing classes to drive two hours and fifteen minutes to slip on her stilettos and a slinky dress and parade around for her stepbrother's clients. No desire to end Wednesday evening on her knees, no matter the cash Ryan might hand her when the night was over.

It irked her that she had repeatedly told Ryan and Luke no, that she hadn't gone home to work a party for them in months, but they still called.

She managed to look Janie in the eyes every day at work and smile and talk to her as if everything was still good, as if Blaize Stewart hadn't kissed her and dragged up a lot of unwanted memories and feelings. Janie invited her to grab a quick dinner at their house Tuesday between work and class, so she'd dropped in and scarfed down two tacos and a bottle of water. Evan was still a little testy about the previous weekend, but he had cooled off from aggressively angry to petulant. It did cross her mind that she could win him over if she had five minutes alone with him in the closet, but with the boys around, she couldn't blow his lingering irritation away.

When she was ready to leave, though, with her keys in hand, Evan had shocked her. Dragged her into the pantry and pulled the door closed. The kiss was hot and wet and long—so long that Konnor tried to pull away more than once, afraid his sons would have a craving for potato chips and come looking in the pantry. He hadn't said a word when he finally released her. Simply opened the door and ushered her out, as if they had been in the pantry with the door closed looking for a particular can of peas. Janie was on the phone—she'd waved at Konnor, a smile on her face—but neither of the boys was around.

While Konnor loved kissing Evan—funny, really, because before Evan she hadn't been into kissing—it was still Blaize's kiss that kept coming back to her at inopportune times. Like when she was sitting in Macro-Economics and trying to pay attention. When she was counting money out to a customer at the teller line. When Evan was kissing her. Evan's kisses were sometimes soft and playful, but mostly, they were greedy and demanding, and something inside Konnor soared to life knowing she had that effect on him.

But Blaize's kiss had been so tentative, so careful, and then so tender, something inside her was still craving more of that.

Ryan called on Wednesday when party time rolled around and she wasn't there. She silenced her phone for class, but she saw the missed call when she got home. She didn't bother listening to his message, let alone calling him back.

Thursday, Janie asked her to come for dinner on Saturday. No scarfing down tacos. No three-way sex upstairs, either, since the boys would be home. But an actual hang-out-for-a-while, sit-down-and-talk dinner. Konnor usually loved hanging out at their house for adult activities and family activities. But she wasn't excited about going this time, and that bothered her. Worse, they would notice.

She didn't hate her night classes, but she was ready to get done with this part of her life. Three weeks ago, she turned twenty-seven, and she was still a part-time college student, with a part time job, thinking about her future. Konnor was ready to fast forward and be in her future. Working. Full time. In a field she loved. Sure, she wanted to be a business owner, but she would be thrilled just to be in the full-time work force, learning through experience rather than books and lectures.

It was nice having something to do in the evenings, though, she decided as she parked her Malibu at the curb in front of her apartment. Not that she liked going to class every night, but if she didn't have class, she might end up sitting at home alone all night, every night. Or at Janie and Evan's every night, and that was such a pathetic thought, she squelched it immediately.

She grabbed her backpack from the passenger seat, climbed out of her car, and swung the door closed. Konnor was a summer kind of girl, but she liked fall okay, and the closer it got to Halloween, the better she liked it. No particular reason. She didn't have big exciting memories from her childhood that made her love Halloween. Nothing remarkably good or bad. She just loved the crisp, clean air, the changing leaves, and pumpkin bread.

Nothing wrong with a good Halloween scare, either. In fact, she decided as she trotted up the steps around the house, she would find a horror movie on TV tonight and settle in on the couch. She'd had a salad for dinner between work and her class, so maybe she would even splurge and have some popcorn.

The dark shadow at the top of the steps made her jump so hard, she almost plunged backwards down the steps. Blaize's hand reached for her and curled around her forearm. His firm grasp might have been comforting if he wasn't such a rat for what he had said to her last weekend. Right after he kissed her, just before he walked away from her.

Besides, she had *wobbled* on the steps. She wasn't going to fall.

"What are you doing here?" She jerked her arm away and squeezed by him.

"Waiting for you."

"Why up here? Why are you camped out by my door?"

"Figured this was a nice neighborhood, and I might look suspicious if I hung out in my car waiting."

"And creeping up the steps to my apartment and sitting in the dark isn't suspicious?"

"I didn't creep," he argued.

Konnor rolled her eyes as she stepped up to the door and stuck the key in the lock.

"You could've just called," she mumbled. "What do you want, anyway?"

"I don't have your number, and neither one of your brothers would give it to me."

"Whadda ya know?" She popped the lock and pushed the door open. Truthfully, she wasn't surprised Luke and Ryan hadn't given Blaize her number. They wouldn't want her to be any more distracted from the job they wanted her to be doing than she already was. "What do you want, Blaize?"

"Can I come in?"

"No."

"Really?"

The streetlight out in front of the brick bungalow lit up the sidewalk and porch out front, but the light was faded and silvery back here, like a poor quality black and white photograph. Still, Konnor could see the look of disbelief on his face as he stood on the rooftop staring at her.

"We have to have this conversation out here?"

"Nope." She shrugged. "We don't have to have any conversations, Blaize."

She stepped inside, but he didn't move when she swung the door closed. Konnor hissed with frustration as she eyed him through the glass pane.

"What?" She tugged the door open and rested her head on the frame. "Why are you bothering me?"

"Do you have plans?" He sounded guarded now. Konnor watched the mask slide over his face. He was worried about Evan and Janie showing up again. Or, maybe he thought she entertained other married couples, and someone different might show up tonight.

"I do." She nodded.

"Konnor." He clenched his teeth and looked away.

"Here's what I'm gonna do. I'm gonna close the door, because I don't wanna talk to you. And I'm gonna put on sweats and pop some popcorn and find a scary movie on TV and forget that you showed up again."

"Scary movies are better with friends."

"Maybe." She shrugged. "Don't have any around right

now."

"We were friends." His gruff reminder drew a shiver from somewhere deep inside. Konnor rubbed her hands up over her arms, hating that he noticed. He held her gaze when she met his eyes.

"Maybe," she said again. "But we aren't anymore."

"Why?"

"Blaize."

"Why aren't we friends now, Konnor?"

She licked her lips, eyes glued to his, hating the memories that roared through her mind again. The things she'd done in her stepbrothers' rooms. The way the boys had pawed at her. Grunted as they rutted around between her legs, trying to figure out what to do with their dicks. Others watching them. Blaize always studiously avoiding the scene.

The night she had found him alone in the kitchen and moved closer to him, wanting just one kiss.

"Goodnight." She started to close the door again, but this time, Blaize put his hand up to stop her. He didn't shove the door open. Didn't sneer or insult her. Simply met her eyes again and waited. "Dammit." She stepped back and turned away, letting him decide if following her inside was worth her anger.

"Where were you? Earlier?"

The apartment was big, and even the kitchen was big enough, but Konnor found herself standing in near darkness, toe to toe with him.

"Class, Blaize." She flipped on the light, moved to put space between them, and set her backpack on the table. "I work. Go to school. Life. Remember that? I have one."

"What class? Tonight?"

"Accounting."

"Do you like it?"

"Why are you here?" she snapped. "Why are you in my

face again? Asking me stupid questions? Why are you here, Blaize?"

"I'm definitely gonna be working with the city," he mumbled. "They hired me as a consultant on the clinic project."

She shrugged and tossed her hands up. "So?"

"So, I'll be living here temporarily."

"'Kay." She nodded. "Go make new friends, because I don't want you here."

"Why not?"

"Seriously?"

"Yeah, seriously. Did we have some big blowout when we were kids? Something I don't remember?"

Konnor stared at him silently. When he didn't move, when his expression didn't change from the look of genuine confusion, she shook her head and stalked out of the room. Blaize followed her.

"Stop." She turned back to him at the door to her bedroom. "I'm gonna change clothes."

"Konnor."

"I know. You've seen it all before, and I could take it all off right now and interest you about as much as the lamp in the living room does, but I'd rather you not just waltz into my bedroom like you belong here."

Gaze locked with hers, Blaize huffed out a long-suffering sigh. His eyes took a long, slow walk down over her shoulders and breasts—covered by a plain gray t-shirt bra and an old Nirvana t-shirt—and her long denim-clad legs, and then trekked back up, pausing again for just a moment at her breasts. Damned her body for taking notice. Her nipples grew stiff, though, thankfully there was no way Blaize could know that.

When he met her eyes again, heat pooled between her legs. She told herself it was simply that she knew he wasn't interested. It was the quest, the chase. And not being able to conquer him all these years. There was no other reason for her body to react that way from how he had just sized her up.

"I'm not leaving."

He spoke so quietly, stayed so still, for a moment Konnor thought she imagined the words. When he parted his lips, her eyes were drawn to them, but no way in hell would she put her mouth on his again.

"Suit yourself," she mumbled. She backed away from the door, though she left it open. Blaize's shoulders lifted as he pulled in a deep breath, and then all in one motion, he shrugged out of his jacket and turned to give her some privacy. She stood motionless at the foot of her bed until he was out of sight.

When she heard the tell-tale squeak of the couch springs, she stripped out of her jeans and pulled on a pair of soft white sweatpants. She hesitated for just a moment, because the last damned thing she wanted was for him to think she was making a play for him. But she quickly worked her bra off while still wearing her shirt, in case he decided to come back and check on her.

As if.

He might walk back down the hall blindfolded, but he wasn't going to come nosing around hoping for a peek at any skin. She tossed her bra to the end of the bed and then slipped into the bathroom to check her breasts in the T-shirt. She was vain enough that they had to look good, but not so perky or bouncy or nipply that she looked like she was trying to turn him on.

"So, what movie were you planning to watch?" he asked when she walked back through the living room.

"I don't know." She didn't even look his way when she crossed through to the kitchen.

"I found something called *Zombie Freeway*," he called.

"*Zombie Freeway*?" she mumbled as she rummaged in her tiny pantry for popcorn. "Isn't that a kids' cartoon?"

"What?"

She jumped when she heard Blaize's voice directly behind her.

"You sure you wanna watch something scary?" He quirked an eyebrow at her when she looked at him over her shoulder. "You're pretty jumpy as it is."

"I'm not used to finding random strangers in the dark by my door." She turned away from him again, though she'd found the popcorn. He stood too close to her, making her think about the kiss with Evan in the Bellinger pantry the other night. Making her wish things were different, and she had her own guy to kiss wherever she wanted, whenever she wanted.

Not that that guy should be Blaize.

"And I'm not used to sharing my space with someone else."

"C'mon, K." He touched her shoulder. Just a quick rub, not even skin to skin contact. "I'm not a random stranger. I helped you write out all the lyrics to that song in that *Mary Poppins* movie. And then I listened to you sing it for days straight."

Konnor snorted and rolled her eyes.

"I've never regretted anything so much in my life."

He was grinning when she finally twisted around to look at him.

"I put up with your obsession with that one Nintendo game for months."

Rather than deter him, he gave her a grand shrug and a nod. "We're not strangers."

"Look, I was serious earlier. I work. I go to classes. Now and then I go out after class on Wednesday nights. It's not too exciting, Blaize. If you're coming to Rockfield to live for a while, why start here? Go find new, exciting people to talk to."

"I'd rather get to know you again," he said simply.

"Back up." She pushed at him, because he hadn't given an inch, and if she moved at all, they would be pressed together again like they were last weekend. When he kissed her.

"You live here alone?" he asked as he stepped back to give her room.

"Didn't I tell you that already?"

"Is the rent high?"

"It's not really that bad," she answered. She pulled the microwave door open and put the popcorn bag inside. "Why? Are you going to ask me what I'm using the cash from Ryan and Luke for?"

"Well, no, that's not where I was going." He rested on the counter at his back. "But since you brought it up." He shrugged and tipped his head expectantly.

"Do you know I don't do that anymore?"

Blaize opened his mouth to answer her, but he hesitated. "I'm not sure what you're saying."

Eyes locked, the memories of the past threaded between them, Konnor flinched.

"I've only been back home a few times this year."

"You were pretty high demand."

"Wow." She turned to punch in the settings on the microwave and kept her back to him.

"You always were, K."

"Can we not talk about this?"

"Are you quitting the parties?"

Yes, she was. But she was moving on from that part of her life for herself, not for anyone else. Sure as hell not for a guy. Any guy. A rush of defensiveness, of anger, climbed her throat, but she swallowed it. Shrugged without comment.

"Let me live here with you."

"No."

"I'll pay the rent. I'll buy the groceries. I'll shovel snow in the winter. Whatever—"

"No."

"Why not?"

"Why?" she snapped. She whirled around now to stare him down. "Why would you even suggest that? You just walked through the whole place, Blaize. Did you see a guest room?"

"No."

"Well, I know you're not interested in fucking me in my bed, but you're not gonna toss out rent money so you can sleep in my bed." She shrugged.

"You don't know me."

He spoke so quietly, Konnor was afraid she didn't hear him correctly. She knew he wouldn't repeat himself, so she didn't give him the satisfaction of asking him to.

"You have a couch."

"I sit there for an hour, and my body hurts. You wanna live here and sleep on that?"

"You care about my comfort?"

"Rockfield has some really cool new condos. Some great apartments downtown. All newly renovated. They would be even closer to your job site. If you live here, we'll be at each other's throats, and I don't really need that kind of stress right now."

Really, she didn't need the reminder of the one that got away. No, the one who walked away. The one who watched her blow all of his buddies and screw a few of his buddies when all she only ever wanted was to be with him.

"Will you let me stay until I find a place?"

She deflated. When the microwave beeped, she yanked

the door open so hard, she almost swung it back far enough to crack her knuckles on the next cabinet.

"Is it because you're involved with them? Or is...that... your new thing? You...with married couples? Like, do you guys...are they here sometimes? Do you work here now?"

Konnor froze, hands in the air—one still on the door handle and the other on the microwave itself—and hung her head.

"Because we can figure out a system. Like if you leave the kitchen light on or if—"

At least he hadn't just suggested he sit out in the living room while she entertained Janie and Evan—or other married couples—in her bedroom.

"Whatever." Emotion made her throat ache, and it hurt to speak, and the whole argument had left her limp and used, and she didn't want the damned popcorn, or the movie, or Blaize.

"You'll let me stay?"

"Sure." She shrugged as she dropped the popcorn on the stovetop. She closed the microwave door and took a deep breath. "I'm not hungry now. And I have some reading to do for class, so." She turned to look at him and shrugged. "Help yourself."

"Konnor." He followed her when she left the room. But again, she stopped at her bedroom to keep him in the hallway.

"If you're gonna stay here, you buy your food. You do your own laundry. And you pick up after yourself."

"Konnor."

"And stay out of my space." She closed the door in his face. Her bag was in the other room. She didn't have what she needed to read for class. Her phone was in her bag. It wasn't even ten o'clock. But she wasn't leaving her bedroom until morning.

5

Thankfully, Konnor still had a plain old alarm clock in her bedroom. So, even though she had a rough night for sleep, she was awake at six. Feeling more tired than when she went to bed, she slipped out of her room and into the bathroom. Her shoulders hurt, and her left side hurt, and it hit her when she finished in the bathroom and made her way to the kitchen that she'd slept curled up tight in a ball, with her back to the door.

Because of Blaize.

When in all reality, she could sleep in the nude with no sheet covering her, and he wouldn't be tempted to waltz in on her. She could have closed her eyes last night and touched herself and thought about Evan or Janie and made all kinds of sexy noises in her room, and Blaize wouldn't have noticed.

She glanced at the couch. Felt a mix of relief and disappointment when she realized Blaize wasn't there. Well, that was weird. She didn't want him here, so why would she feel that little niggle of let down at seeing him gone? Maybe because if she had known he left, she would have relaxed and slept better.

But the smell of coffee hit her at the same time she realized the kitchen light was on. That little inkling of disappointment whooshed away with a flash of frustration. She wondered how long he planned to stay, because the emotions at war inside her were already killing her after one night.

"Hey." He offered her a tentative smile. Konnor eyed him silently, all the frustration and uncertainty falling away at the sight of a bedhead, sleepy-looking Blaize at her table with a laptop open in front of him. He'd changed clothes last night; the jeans and long-sleeved shirt were gone. Konnor reminded herself not to stare at his bare legs, at the hint of strong, lean thighs under his athletic shorts. At his bare feet. At the soft gray shirt that sculpted a delicious-looking chest and shoulders.

"Good morning." He stood, and damned her eyes for ignoring her brain and sliding down over his chest—pecs outlined just so in the tight-fitting shirt—his belly, where the tail of his shirt rode up and exposed solid-looking abs and the feathering of dark hair that led straight to the good stuff in his shorts. "Want some coffee?"

Her eyes jumped from his crotch to his face. Embarrassed that he had caught her checking him out, even though she was only mimicking his crude behavior from the night before, she scowled and turned to get it herself.

"I'll get it." He picked up the mug he was using, and Konnor watched him drink from it, fascinated by his hands around her mug, drinking coffee at her apartment at this early hour. She'd had plenty of daydreams about this morning for years—before she finally put her stupid crush behind her—but they all involved a better night than she'd had last night.

"What time do you have to be at work?" he asked her. Konnor breathed deeply to inhale the scent of coffee and watched him pour her a cup. Evan made coffee for her and

Janie in the mornings after they'd all had a rare night together. She figured he made coffee for Janie and breakfast for Janie and probably made love to Janie on the kitchen table when it was just the two of them.

Her hands were shaking slightly when she took the mug from Blaize.

"K?"

"I clock in around ten 'til eight." Her voice was low and scratchy, and she realized suddenly that she'd cried a little bit last night when she went to bed. Because she was used to living alone, she hadn't paid attention to her reflection in the mirror in the bathroom. She didn't give a damn if her hair was messy, but she didn't want to broadcast to Blaize that she had been upset when she went to bed.

"Want breakfast?" he offered.

Because her mind went straight to the last thought she'd had about Evan and Janie and the kitchen table, she turned her back to Blaize and sat at the dinette.

"No."

"I was going to make an omelet, but I thought you might like one, too."

She glanced at his laptop. From her angle, she couldn't see it well, but it looked like he had a local realtor's page up.

"I don't." She shook her head, but Blaize moved around her kitchen now like he owned it. He whipped up an omelet the size of a small throw pillow and then cut it in half. Toasted bread and then carried it all to the table. "Blaize, I don't eat breakfast."

"Well, you should," he answered. She watched him gather the butter and utensils and napkins and return to the table to sit with her. "My wife always said I was better in the kitchen than the bedroom."

Konnor rested her elbows on the table, ignored the food, and stared at him silently.

"What?" He forked a big bite of the omelet, drawing Konnor's attention to the cheese and bell peppers oozing out the sides. "I didn't poison it. Eat."

"Your wife?" Her voice was husky with emotion, and she hated her damned stupid teenage heart, alive and well in her chest.

"Ex-wife." He shrugged. "Maybe that's why she divorced me."

"Because you force fed her breakfast?" she asked softly.

"Because I was better in the kitchen than the bedroom."

Konnor pressed her lips together and lowered her gaze to the food. Her stomach was going to growl, but she wasn't sure it was hunger. Very possible it was that knot of conflicting emotions in the pit of her belly making her feel funny.

"Maybe you are gay," she said quietly. "If you had trouble getting it up for her."

"Wow." He laughed, but she heard the bitter note in the outburst. "I just fixed you breakfast, and you slam me like that first thing in the morning?"

She shrugged her eyebrows and took another drink of her coffee.

"I didn't ask you to fix me breakfast," she reminded him.

"Damn, K, you're a ball breaker."

"You've pretty much always known that, Blaize."

"I didn't say I couldn't get it up for her." He shrugged at Konnor. "She said I was better in the kitchen than the bedroom."

"I didn't know you were married."

"You didn't ask."

"What happened?"

"I don't think anything happened." He focused on his laptop, reading or pretending to read something. "So much as we just rushed into something that wasn't the real thing."

"Do you have kids?" She picked up her fork, but she hesitated. She hated him right at this particular moment. For never wanting to be with her, sure. But because he'd had something. He had a wife and a career, and even though he didn't now, it was more than Konnor had ever allowed herself.

"No." He cleared his throat. "Kristi was pregnant when we got married. But, she lost the baby."

Guilt zapped her in the heart.

"I'm sorry," she said sincerely. Blaize only nodded, eyes still on the laptop. Konnor shoveled a bite of the omelet to her mouth in a lame attempt to convey her sympathy. But the cheesy egg and pepper mixture was hot and tasty, and her hunger trumped the riot in her belly.

"I found a few spots that look okay," he told her. Konnor studied his face in the bright yellow overhead light. His eyes looked bloodshot, the skin around them bruised and puckered. He probably hadn't slept well on the couch, but he looked bedraggled and worn to the bone. "I'll call them when the offices open and see if I can set up a walk through—"

"Don't rush," she mumbled. "It's not that big of a deal."

Blaize lifted his gaze from the screen to look at her. "I don't want your pity, Konnor."

"It's not pity," she argued. "I envy you. I have a lot of feelings about you, Blaize Stewart, but pity isn't one of them."

"You envy me?"

She took another bite of her omelet and then remembered she hadn't charged her phone before she went to bed. Blaize watched her dig through her backpack on the seat next to her and then pull her phone out to look at it. Konnor ignored him, eyes on her screen. She'd missed a call from a girl in her Macro class. Probably about an assignment. She had two missed calls from Janie.

And a text from Evan.

Janie has plans with girlfriends tonight.

Konnor felt a rush of heat pool between her legs. Evan was asking to see her. The nice thing about their relationship was that Janie would know he had texted her. If Konnor and Evan were together tonight at his house or here, Janie wouldn't mind. Konnor had needed this; she'd been hoping for alone time with Evan for a while now. But the bad thing about their relationship was that even if she and Evan had a perfect night, there was a time limit. He would go back to being Janie's husband, and Konnor would be alone. Same as always.

Blaize cleared his throat. Konnor lifted only her eyes to look at him.

"I can leave," he told her. "Tonight. If you…" He nodded to her phone.

"Did you read my texts?"

"No, but I can read the look on your face," he answered.

Konnor was torn. She wanted to see Evan. But staring at Blaize's handsome face—the years looked too damned good on him—only reminded her of the heartache of unrequited love. Even if Evan loved her, he could never love her enough. Because he could never be free of Janie.

I can't tonight, Ev.

She tapped out her response and set her phone screen down on the table.

"How does it work?" Blaize asked gruffly. He rubbed his eyes and then smoothed his hand over the scruff on his cheek.

Konnor simply stared at him.

"I'm curious. Is it always the three of you at the same time? Are there other couples?"

"No." She swallowed hard.

"Is it ever just you and her?"

"Does that turn you on?" She tipped her head.

"Is that why you do it? To turn other people on?"

That was exactly why she used to do the things she did. But times had changed. *She* had changed.

"I'm gonna go take a shower." She climbed to her feet. "Thank you for breakfast."

———

"SO, THIS IS HOW IT STARTS," Evan reminded her. Konnor, phone at her ear, rolled her eyes as she dashed up the steps to her apartment. She didn't know what kind of car Blaize drove, but she hadn't noticed any that looked out of place when she parked out front.

"Ev." She unlocked her door, stepped inside, and slipped her flats off.

"He's been in town for a week," Evan told her. "And now you're telling me you can't see me tonight."

"He hasn't been *here* all week," she argued. "And he's not here now."

"Then what're you doing tonight?"

"Nothing," she whispered.

"Do you know how long it's been since we've had time alone? Not party sex, but real alone time?" Evan asked her. She dropped her purse on the couch as she made her way to her bedroom. Phone still pressed to her ear, she shimmied out of her slacks and found a pair of yoga pants to tug on.

"Evan." She swallowed hard. "Today at work, Janie told everyone you guys are planning a trip to Cabo for your anniversary."

"We are."

"I can't make love with you tonight after that."

"You're jealous? Now?"

"Well, yeah, I am, but it just hit me again how weird this is. You guys have a life that doesn't involve me—"

"Do you wanna go to Cabo with us?"

A few weeks ago, Konnor might have loved the idea. Now it hurt that he would even ask her.

"No." She perched on the edge of her bed and unbuttoned her blouse. "Don't be so obtuse, Ev. I want someone to whisk *me* away to the beach for sand and sun and fruity drinks. I want someone to reach for me in the morning. Not his wife and then me. I want what you and Janie have."

"Is he feeding you this stuff? Telling you what we're doing is wrong?"

"No."

"Because you were happy with what we were doing until he showed up."

"Evan."

"I was going to bring your favorite wine. Chocolate covered strawberries. And I was going to lick you all over while you laid back and enjoyed it. I dreamt about the way you feel on my tongue, Kon."

Her eyes burned with tears. She heard the door open and close and fought a tiny thrill that Blaize had come back.

"I'm sorry."

Evan groaned and sighed, clearly frustrated with her.

"Are you coming to dinner tomorrow night?"

"Yes."

"Are you fucking him tonight?'

"Evan—"

She dropped her phone to her bed when Evan cut the call off. Miserable and all of her own making, she sat with her head in her hands and let the tears slide. When Blaize tapped on her bedroom door, she jumped to her feet and turned her back to him.

"Hey. K. What's wrong?"

She shook her head and swiped at her eyes. "Nothing."

"Look, I have an appointment to look at an apartment."

His voice was much too close for him to be in the hall outside the room. "I'll be out of here over the weekend. In fact, I can get a hotel room—"

"It's fine." She swallowed hard. "I don't care. If you stay."

"Were you…just on the phone?"

Forgetting that she'd been in the process of changing clothes, she turned to him. Blaize's eyes roamed low, down over her parted blouse. She nodded, though with his eyes on her breasts, she doubted he saw her. Feeling reckless, angry with Evan and even more so with herself, she shrugged out of the blouse and tossed it to the bed. Blaize's eyes roamed up to meet hers and then back to her breasts, covered in purple lace.

"What're you doing?"

She found a t-shirt in her top drawer and reached back to unhook her bra.

"K?"

"You're in my bedroom, Blaize. I'm changing clothes."

Eyes on him, she slipped the bra off and let it drop to the floor at her feet. Blaize jerked his gaze up to look her in the eye.

"Put a shirt on, Konnor," he pleaded. "You're killing me."

Disappointed, hurt, embarrassed, Konnor pulled the shirt over her head and then marched around him to leave the bedroom. She needed to drink. She wanted the hard stuff. Whiskey. Evan— sort of. But she wanted, she needed, Evan on her own terms, and it was out of the question. She would never hurt Janie that way, but she was tired of being the one hurting in their unconventional relationship. She needed Blaize, but clearly, he wasn't remotely attracted to her.

It killed her to know he had been married. To think of him sliding into bed with the same woman night after night. Sliding into the same *woman*, night after night. Touching her. Sleeping with his arms around her. Fixing her breakfast.

In the kitchen, she splashed a finger of bourbon in a glass and sipped it. Raised her eyes to scowl at Blaize when he joined her.

"Do you wanna go with me?"

"No."

"You have plans for the night?" He hesitated at the door but finally continued into the room until he stood much too close to her. Again.

"No."

"Konnor, I'm sorry."

"For what?"

"I dunno. Whatever's going on in that head."

She laughed bitterly. "I don't want your pity, Blaize."

She pulled away and threw her head back when he stepped closer to her and kissed her. His lips were warm and soft and just what she needed. Except not really. Kissing him might feel good now, but no matter what happened, she would end up miserable. She'd rather overindulge on the bourbon and deal with the devil she knew.

"Don't." She turned her head when he flicked his tongue over her parted lips and lapped at the middle of her upper lip. He didn't stop. Instead, he eased his tongue between her teeth until he touched hers. "Blaize."

"You can't show me your breasts and think it's not gonna make me fuckin' crazy, K."

"I don't want a pity fuck." She pushed at him, but he wouldn't budge.

"What makes you think this is pity?"

"You've never been interested before," she reminded him. "Why would that suddenly change?"

Konnor watched him boldly, though she regretted the words the moment they were out of her mouth Now that she'd said it, though, she wanted, needed, him to respond. To acknowledge the fact that he had never been interested in being with her.

"Come with me."

"What?"

"Come with me," he said again.

"That's all you have to say to me?" She swallowed hard and lowered her gaze. "After all these years, that's all you have to say?"

"K." Blaize curled his fingers around her forearm and used his other hand to pry the glass from her grip. Konnor turned her head when he leaned in around her to put the glass on the counter. "I want you to come with me."

She closed her eyes when he pressed his cheek to her head and stroked his fingers up over her arm. Afraid of what might slip out of her mouth, of the truths her heart might throw out for him to hear, she bit her lip, but when he moved to nuzzle her neck, she tipped her head.

Blaize cupped her chin in his hand and held her steady for another kiss. The liquor had burned a trail down her throat and chased a pleasant warmth through her body. The heat of Blaize's kiss followed the same trail. Forgetting that she was angry with him for barging back into her life and for not being attracted to her when they were kids and longing for Evan and being angry with Evan, Konnor kissed him back. His tongue was warm and gentle, the kiss slow, tender the way she remembered it from the other day.

Everything she told Evan she didn't do. Everything Evan had taught her to love.

Forgetting that Blaize didn't want her, that he was placating her, and even if he did want a piece, he would never love her the way she wanted to be loved, she lifted her hands and settled them ever so gently on his shoulders. When he didn't stop kissing her, she allowed her hands to slide up over the back of his neck. She tangled her fingers in the back of his hair and groaned out loud when he pulled away from her.

"Come with me," he said again. "Be my date tonight."

The second he let go of her chin, she tucked it to her chest and shook her head.

"I'm not big on dating," she mumbled.

"We can see the apartment. Grab dinner. And catch up."

"I think we did that already, Blaize," she reminded him. "This morning. When you told me about your wife."

"I want to be with you." His voice was gruff. "I want to hang out with you, K."

"Janie has plans tonight," she whispered. "Which means Evan and I could have the night together."

"She doesn't mind?"

"No."

Blaize backed away from her and shoved his hands in his hip pockets.

"So, you can stand here and kiss me like that and then go climb into his bed?"

"No." She lifted her chin and met his eyes.

"I don't get it." He offered her a dramatic shrug. "You deserve so much more than that."

"No, I don't," she argued.

Clearly frustrated, Blaize hung his head and sighed. "Okay. I'll get out of your way. Maybe we can…" He looked at her and shook his head. "Maybe we can get a drink sometime."

She watched him turn away. When he was two steps from the door, she realized he was really going to leave.

"Blaize."

He stopped, but he stood with his back to her.

"I told him no."

"You told him no?"

"I told him I couldn't see him tonight."

"Because of me?"

"Does it matter why? I told him no."

He turned to her slowly. For just a moment, Konnor saw that same exhaustion on his face that she'd seen this morning. She wondered how long he had been divorced. How long he was married. If he had wanted the baby they lost.

"So, come with me."

Konnor sighed and nodded. "Okay."

Blaize stalked back across the room to stand next to her.

"Do me one favor?"

"What?"

"Put a bra on, because it's still making me crazy knowing how easy it would be touch you right now."

His words hurt badly enough, but the fact that he couldn't look her in the eyes when he said them took her breath away. Why couldn't he just touch her right now? Blaize was divorced. Konnor had just confessed to telling Evan no; there was nothing stopping them from being together.

"Fine." She nodded and slipped by him to leave the room.

Konnor went to the bathroom first. She splashed cold water on her face and then patted it dry before looking in the mirror. Right about now, she needed a friend to talk her through the heartache, not another lover to add to it.

6

The rental house was a dump, and Konnor actually laughed with Blaize at the rundown building that was so small it would fit inside her living room. Blaize had reached for her hand to steady her as they walked over a hole in the front porch to get inside the place. Even with the anger, the sadness, still welling inside, she cherished the moment of hand holding and wished it would last longer. But once inside, as they followed the realtor around the dark, forlorn space, Blaize let go of her hand, and Konnor shoved hers in her pockets. She'd changed from yoga pants to jeans when she put her bra on, deciding if she was going to send Blaize back out to the world again, she should at least try to make him regret what he was missing. Yoga pants and a faded old T-shirt weren't too attractive on her, but the skinny jeans and green sweater at least looked like she'd made an effort.

Evan liked the sweater, said it made her eyes pop, and there was some bizarre thing inside her that loved carrying that knowledge around while she was with Blaize.

"Did you see the rust in that sink?" he asked as they

settled back into his truck. Konnor clicked her seatbelt and took one last look at the rental.

"The sink?" She looked back at him with wide eyes. "Blaize, did you see how the back door was falling off the hinges?"

He started the truck, shot her a grin, and shrugged. "It looked good in the pictures."

"Was it the same house?"

His laughter was better than music, and for a second, Konnor felt good. Normal. Like a girl out on a date with a guy she liked.

"Yes. The pictures had that gross pea green carpet."

"You just said it looked good in the pictures."

"Well, other than that." He dropped the truck in gear and glanced at her again. "Hungry?"

She wasn't, but she didn't want the night to end. The walk through of the rental house had only taken twenty-five minutes, and Konnor hated the thought of Blaize dumping her back at her place and taking off to find a hotel room. She was a little bit afraid that she would cave and call Evan, a little bit afraid Evan would ignore her call, but mostly, she knew she would sit at home alone. And after experiencing a small slice of a relationship with someone, alone now meant lonely.

"Sure."

"Sure?" He tipped his head at her, calling her on the fib, but he drove away from the rental without further comment. "Tell me where to go. What's good?"

"What're you hungry for?" She relaxed back in her seat and eyed the familiar sites as Blaize navigated the streets. She had been in Rockfield for a good ten months now, and it was beginning to feel like home. Would she feel the need to run if she ended things with the Bellingers? She didn't want to lose them—as friends—but even more than that, she didn't want to lose the life she'd built here.

"How about a burger?"

"Go to Buck and Quarter," she told him.

"Like the food is a buck and a quarter?"

At the next stoplight, he frowned at her, suspicious of her food choice.

"Nope. The guy who owns it is named Buck. Calvin Buck. His dog's name is Quarter."

"You're bullshitting me."

"I'm not." She shook her head.

"Tell me where to turn," he told her. The smirk on his face told her he was enjoying himself, teasing her. She directed him back into the heart of town and then west a few blocks to the bar and grill situated in a refurbished warehouse. When he parked, Konnor glanced at her phone to check the time. She noticed a text from Evan, but she refused to let her eyes scroll down the screen past the time. Not quite seven.

"Will it be crowded?" Blaize looked around the packed parking lot.

"The bar will be," she told him as they climbed down from the truck. She led him down the sidewalk to the front door. "But I don't think it'll be tough to get a table."

Inside, the golden lights lent the place a warm, welcoming atmosphere. Several people gathered at the bar, and a bunch more milled about the tables in the vicinity of the bar. Konnor noticed the corner booth was empty, so she led Blaize to the table and scooted in to sit on the far side. The upright wooden booths weren't the most comfortable—Buck told people if they wanted to loiter, to belly up to the bar and leave the booths for customers who were dining—but they did offer a quiet, private experience.

"Did you bring me here so no one would see you with me?"

Konnor met his eyes over the table and tipped her head. "Why would I do that?"

"Because you're involved with someone else."

"Well, it's not like anyone outside of me and Janie and Evan know that."

"Why do you settle for that?"

She dismissed his concern with a shrug. Country music surrounded them, though it wasn't so loud as to inhibit comfortable conversation.

"Why would you envy me?"

Konnor stared at him silently and sighed with relief when the waitress approached with menus. The woman—probably their age—was friendly, obviously smitten with Blaize, though thankfully, she didn't fawn over him or call him *hon*. Both of them ordered draft beers. Konnor watched the waitress walk away, but she felt the heat of Blaize's stare.

"K? You didn't answer me."

Without a word, she swung her gaze back to meet his eyes.

"Why would you envy me?"

"Because you got married." She shrugged. Wished she had her beer so she could hide behind the glass. "Because you were expecting a baby."

"We lost the baby," he reminded her. "And Kristi and I weren't right for each other."

"Did you have a big wedding?"

"Mmm." He shrugged his lips. "Define big. No. Not really. It was nice. Pretty. She was a beautiful bride. She had three bridesmaids. Her niece was our flower girl."

"Did everyone know? That she was pregnant?"

"No." He spread his fingers out on the table and studied them. Konnor wondered what his hand looked like with a wedding ring on it. She figured she wouldn't like the look too much. "She wasn't showing yet. Lost the baby at the end of the first trimester."

"I can't imagine."

"She was sad." Blaize nodded. "Hurting. I was disappointed, but I think at that stage, it was harder for her. It wasn't real enough for me yet. I went with her to her doctor appointments and stuff, but I wasn't *carrying* a baby inside me. I wanted the baby, but I wasn't connected enough yet."

Konnor licked her lips. She nodded but waited when the waitress approached with their beers to speak again. Blaize asked for a burger; Konnor asked for a plate of fries and avoided his frown when the woman walked away again.

"That's all you're gonna eat?"

She sipped her beer. "Don't have much of an appetite right now."

"I still don't get—"

"You had everything I'll never get a chance at," she mumbled. "You lost it. But you had it. I'll never know what that's like."

"Losing someone?"

"Loving someone. Exchanging vows." She put her glass down and smoothed her fingers over her temples.

"Why wouldn't you?"

"Who's gonna marry me, Blaize? I'm in the sex business. What guy wants to look at me and think about all the things I've done?"

"You could give it up."

"I'm trying," she answered. "I've told Ry and Luke I'm done. They keep calling. I don't go."

"I hoped that you were happy."

"What?"

"When I came here for the clinic project. The proposal. When I found out you were here, and I decided to look you up, I hoped you were happy."

"I was," she answered. "Maybe not the way you mean, but I was."

"And what happened?"

"How long have you been divorced?" She ignored his question.

"Not quite two years."

"Do you miss her?"

"No," he admitted. "She's with someone else. I wish her well, K. She deserves to be happy. I wasn't going to make her happy. They moved somewhere in Missouri. We don't really stay in touch."

She was itching to check her phone. To see what Evan had said.

"Would you do it again?"

"Get married?" He took a long drink, and Konnor wondered if he did it to borrow time or put her off. "Yeah. I would. But I wouldn't be in such a rush."

"Sometimes," she sighed and continued, "I hate Ryan and Luke."

"For the things that happened?"

"No." She shook her head. "Not really. But for...having normal lives. I don't...I don't blame them for what I did. We were all too young to be doing what we were doing, but we were all old enough to know better, too. I just hate that they're married. That Luke has two little boys. That his wife eyeballs me like she thinks I'm going to molest them. I hate that we were all doing stuff, but I got labeled as the bad girl, and everyone else has a normal life."

"Do you regret any of it?"

Konnor locked eyes with him. "That might be a question best asked after I've had way too much to drink."

"I'm not judging you, K. I'm curious."

"I don't know how to answer you, because I don't want to tell you the truth."

The buzz of her phone drew his attention, but he met her eyes again and waited for her to pick it up. When she didn't, he arched his eyebrows in question.

"I'm sure it's Evan."

"Not gonna look at it?"

"We got into it earlier over the phone."

"Because of me."

She shrugged.

"How did you end up involved with a married couple?"

Konnor took a deep breath and looked around for a rescue. No waitress. Nothing crazy to point out to Blaize to change the subject.

"I don't wanna talk about it, Blaize," she finally mumbled.

"How long has it been going on?"

"A few months."

"I can't imagine sharing my wife with someone else."

Konnor flinched. Maybe he wasn't judging her, but his words, his questions, all dug under her skin and made her bleed.

"You make me regret every damned thing I ever did," she whispered. "I can't stand the way you look at me."

"What does that mean?" he asked quickly.

"The way you've always looked at me."

"Konnor." He leaned over the table and took her hand before she could yank it away from him. She shook her head and tried to offer him a smile.

"If you would have just kissed me." She covered her eyes with her free hand. "If you would have kissed me before… when we were kids."

Blaize stroked his thumb over hers.

"Konnor—"

She shook her head. Her phone buzzed again with a call this time. Blaize withdrew his hand and nodded at it. She picked it up as the waitress returned with their orders.

"Hey, Janie." She cleared her throat and hoped she sounded normal. Not like she was having a stupid emotional meltdown in a bar.

"Kon? Are you okay?"

"I'm fine."

"Ev's upset. Said he said things he shouldn't have. And now you won't answer him."

Blaize had no qualms about listening to her end of the conversation. His eyes were intense as he tore off a big bite of his burger and chewed slowly.

"I'm grabbing dinner with Blaize," Konnor told Janie. "He's been out looking for rental places."

"Okay. I just..." Janie sighed. "Kon, it's okay. If you're ready to...do something different."

Janie's words were meant to soothe her; she knew that, but instead, they were a knife in her throat, and she couldn't breathe.

"Dammit. I'm sorry," Janie rushed on. "I'm sorry. I didn't mean that to sound so cavalier. Sweetheart, I just want you to know that you and I are friends. Girlfriends. It's complicated, I know, because we're sleeping together, and we're sleeping with Evan, but I get that you're young and you want—"

"It's okay," Konnor interrupted her. "I'm okay."

"Do we need to talk about stuff?"

"Maybe."

Blaize's stare still pinned her to the booth.

"Are you still coming to dinner?"

"Yes, I promise I'll be there."

"Bring him."

Konnor laughed softly. "I don't think that's a good idea."

"Maybe it's the best idea."

"I dunno."

"I love you, Kon."

"Me, too." She couldn't say the words back to Janie,

because Blaize was watching her and listening to her. But she saw the heat in his eyes when she said *me, too* and knew that she wasn't hiding anything from him.

"So." He looked away when she put her phone down. She left her hand on it, considered looking at it again to see what Evan had texted her. "Which hotel do you recommend?"

"You don't have to go to a hotel," she said quietly.

"I'm in your way, and it's obvious you're not happy about me being around."

"It's not you," she started.

Blaize chuckled sarcastically. "Really, K? You're gonna blow me off with that line?"

"No. I was gonna say it's not you. It's the way you make me feel about myself that makes me sad. I have a big place, but I'm not sure there's room for you and me and all the regrets."

7

They didn't linger after their dinner, and it had nothing to do with the uncomfortable booth, and everything to do with the uncomfortable vibe between them. Blaize insisted on paying for dinner, though Konnor didn't put up much of an argument. She was ready to lock herself inside her place and carry the bottle of whiskey to the couch and numb all the weird feelings inside. Maybe her mistake was letting Evan and Janie get to her. She should have walked away after that first night with them at Wild Canyon. She'd known she was in dangerous territory, and she'd walked right in, eyes wide open.

Then again, that's how she had always operated.

Slowing down, feeling things with Evan and Janie had left her vulnerable to Blaize. Not that she could have known he would show up all these years later and make her wish she was young again, so she could do things differently.

To her dismay, Blaize parked in front of her place and climbed down from his truck to walk her up.

"You really don't have to do this," she told him as he followed her to the steps.

"I'm not leaving yet," he told her. Maybe he meant the words to be comforting, but she felt the hair on the back of her neck raise with dread. At the top of the steps, she turned to him, but he shook his head and nudged her closer to the door. "You know there's no future for you with what you're doing."

"I told you I don't—"

"It's not anything you've ever done holding you back from happiness, Kon. It's what you're doing now. It's the choices you keep making."

"Blaize."

"You can't be a bride when he has a wife."

"You have no idea what he, what they've, given me."

"I know. I'm just reminding you there's nowhere to go."

She leaned back on the door and folded her arms over her chest.

"And I think you're content to let them break your heart, because at least it's safe. You can't be expected to move forward, to take the next step, when they're married to each other."

Konnor swallowed hard. She wanted to argue with him, to rail at him, and tell him to leave her the hell alone. But he was right. Didn't matter how much she might love either one of them, or how much they might love her, she would never have either of them completely as her own. And as unhappy as that made her, she was letting it continue rather than letting go and looking for happiness on her own.

When he didn't say more, she turned and dug through her purse for her keys.

"You're right," she finally mumbled. "This is just another way for me to hide from what I thought I didn't want."

"When we were kids—"

She stepped inside but turned to him immediately to stop him from following her in.

"Let's just say goodnight, Blaize."

"You scared the hell out of me," he continued. He eased her back, far enough inside that he could close the door. "I mean, we were friends, and that was great. And then suddenly, you were pretty and not just a girl I was friends with."

"You went to homecoming with someone else."

"You were too young."

"It broke my heart."

"When you started taking your clothes off and letting everyone touch you..." He shook his head. "I was scared, Konnor."

"Don't lie to me now," she whispered. "That still hurts, Blaize. The only boy I ever wanted to kiss me couldn't stand to look at me. Don't make it worse now."

"It's not a lie," he promised. "I was scared to death to take my pencil dick out and show it to you. To the whole fuckin' room. I was a skinny runt with a little dick, and I wanted you so fucking bad, I would have come in my jeans if I watched you with the rest of them."

"You think anybody else had anything to brag about?" She laughed humorlessly. "None of them knew what they were doing, and every time I took my clothes off, all I ever wanted was for you to look at me and want me."

"What about now?" Voice gruff, he stepped closer to her. Afraid to touch him, afraid he would vanish again, Konnor backed away. Rather than slipping away from him, she found herself pressed up against the wall with Blaize standing far too close to her for comfort.

"I don't know what you're doing, Blaize." She rested her head on the wall and closed her eyes. "But I know you don't want me."

"Maybe I want more of you than you gave the rest of them."

"Right." She nodded. "You want to get tangled up with me, knowing that Ryan and Luke still call me to help them out at their parties. You want me even though I'm intimately involved with a married couple, who by the way, taught me more about making love than anyone else I've ever been with."

"You could choose me." He shrugged. "Over them. Now."

"And then what?" she whispered. "You and I hook up, and you get bored or you remember who I am and what I've done, and then you move on? You find a new wife, and I'm standing here in the same place? Without you. Without them."

"Sometimes love means risking everything, Konnor."

"Love?" She laughed sarcastically. "Nobody's gonna love me, Blaize."

"What if I do?"

In the dark entry way, Konnor couldn't see Blaize's eyes. But she could feel his nearness, his presence against her. Not leaning, not pushing. Just there. The shape of his lean thighs next to hers. The looming shape of his broad shoulders in front of her. His breath on her face.

"Please don't do this to me." She spoke quietly, but her voice didn't waiver. "You don't have to lie to me to do this. That's only gonna hurt more."

"What if the things I felt for you...when we were younger..." He rested a hand on the wall above her head and leaned closer. Konnor closed her eyes when he brushed a kiss high over her cheekbone. "What if that's why I couldn't love Kristi like I was supposed to?"

"Great." She swallowed hard. "Make me a homewrecker, and I haven't seen you in years."

"We weren't the right fit," he said quietly. "Neither of us was. But maybe you're *my reason* why."

"Maybe you changed your mind and you just wanna fuck

me now, Blaize." She smacked his chest and pushed him away. He groaned, obviously frustrated with her. Konnor walked through the darkness toward her bedroom. "Stay. Go. I don't care. But don't hand me a bunch of lines to ease whatever guilt you feel for wanting to fuck me."

"Dammit, Konnor."

"I'm not stupid," she reminded him. "I've made some questionable decisions, but I'm not stupid."

She flipped her bedroom light on and snatched her pajamas from the bed. Assuming Blaize had headed back toward the door to leave, she jumped when she turned to find him glowering at her from the doorway.

"So, tomorrow night, you're going to dinner at their house."

She stared at him silently. Considered telling him she was going to end it with them. That they might have dinner, and she might kiss them both goodbye, but she knew it was time to move on. She didn't need some hero to swoop in and tell her there was no future in what she was doing.

"Their sons will be there," she mumbled. "It's not like we spend every minute we have together in bed."

"She told you to bring me." He wedged his shoulder on the doorframe.

Konnor laughed softly. "And you want to go? Seriously?"

He stared at her for a long, quiet moment. Feeling fidgety, she unbuttoned her jeans. Anything to get him moving, to get him out of her house. Her life.

"No." He stirred, stepped into her room. "I don't. I don't want to watch you hanging out with them and imagine you in bed with them."

"'kay." She shrugged. She honestly didn't know if she was relieved or disappointed. It would be difficult, tense, to have Blaize there with her. But there was a big part of her heart that desperately wanted to stay in their lives, that needed

Evan and Janie as friends, who wanted them to be around Blaize. She needed Blaize to see that what she had with them wasn't simply a sexual thing. She wasn't just a third person in their bed to liven things up.

She was frustrated, though, that Blaize was still in her bedroom. Eyes on her bed, she unzipped her jeans.

"And don't pull that again." With one big stride, he stood at her side. Konnor stared at his hand silently when he wrapped his fingers around her forearm again.

"What?"

"Don't take your clothes off in front of me, Konnor. Unless you wanna be flat on your back under me, don't do it. I'm not a kid anymore. I'm not afraid of you. And you better fucking believe I wanna lay you down and fuck you."

"Yeah?" She wiggled her jeans down an inch over her hips. "What's stopping you?"

"You are." He shrugged. "I don't share. I don't care how bad I want you, I won't fuck you tonight and send you off to see your other lovers tomorrow night."

She stared after him long after she heard the door slam closed. Her hands trembled as she pushed her jeans down and stepped out of them. In stiff, robotic movements, she put her pajamas on and then treaded back out to the door to lock up. The whole place was still dark. The only trace of Blaize having been there at all was the lingering scent of his cologne in the air. Konnor held her breath when she turned from the door to go back to her room, but it hit her before she was ten steps away.

The one boy she wanted when she was younger had finally come for her. He'd confessed that he wanted to look when they were younger, but he was scared. He'd wondered aloud if maybe one reason his marriage hadn't worked out was because he was a little bit in love with her.

"All these years, Konnor," she whispered. She traipsed

back to the door and peeked out into the night. But the glass pane was cold on her fingertips, and there was no silhouette on the rooftop. Blaize was gone. She didn't even have his number to call him.

The enormity of what she'd just done heavy in her heart, she slid down the wall in the same spot where Blaize had pinned her earlier with just the suggestion of his body against hers.

She might not need a hero to save her from Evan and Janie. She'd known for a while now that she had to walk away from that situation if she were to ever find anything for herself. But if she loved someone, if she loved Blaize Stewart, she needed him here, in her life, didn't she?

———

It took her until late morning to look at her phone, even though she woke up with Blaize on her mind. After a fitful sleep, she finally gave in around eight and let her eyes open and be awake, and then she stared at the ceiling for another hour. Wishing things could have been different. Wishing she would have done things differently when she was a kid. Wishing Blaize would have shown interest in her before now.

Wishing he wouldn't have just shown up here last weekend and thrown her life into chaos. She would be fine; Konnor was always fine. She had come through that whole tainted youth thing mostly unscathed, other than this inability to have real love. She would give herself this morning to wallow in what she just lost again with Blaize. Not a real relationship, not even close. But maybe the possibility of something. She would just lie here and close her eyes and wish he was lying with her, his arm around her waist maybe, and his lips in her hair.

And then she would get up and go on. She had assignments she had to finish. She would clean the apartment and do the laundry. She couldn't have any sheets or blankets that Blaize had used out on the couch still smelling like him. That might make her crazy.

She would grab a bottle of wine to take to the Bellingers' house tonight. And she would have dinner and be herself and have fun with them—all of them, because she loved them all —and then when dinner was over and the boys went their own way, Konnor would tell Evan and Janie she had to end the intimate part of their relationship.

No tears. No waffling. Just say it. If she had to, she would explain that she loved them, but she couldn't just give them so much of herself when she couldn't ask for the same in return. She couldn't hold hands with Evan in public. She would never go out with them—with either of them—as anything other than a friend. And she wasn't part of a Cabo vacation, and that did make her jealous, and worse, it made her angry with herself and them for letting things get so ridiculously out of hand that she could feel jealous of them.

And it wasn't fair that she couldn't have any of that, and she still couldn't have someone to love, someone to love her. Evan had been angry since meeting Blaize last weekend. And Blaize most likely wasn't even *the one*. Evan had promised in the beginning that he understood Konnor was young and would eventually want out for this very reason. It had been Konnor to argue against that idea.

When she did finally look at her phone, she was disappointed to find that Blaize hadn't attempted to get in touch with her. If he wanted to talk to her badly enough, he would find a way to get her number. Surely, he had something on one of her stepbrothers that he could use for blackmail to get her number.

Or he could show up here again, she reminded herself.

Her heart thrilled at the thought, but her brain quickly hammered that idea, that hope, right back down her throat. That right there was her problem. She had let Evan and Janie teach her to hope for things that she knew she didn't deserve. They had given her love, and even though it wasn't the perfect fit for her, she had a taste for it now, and she needed to forget how much she liked it. Craved it.

Time to box those touchy-feely emotions up and put them away. Konnor was level-headed and independent and smart—Evan had made a point of telling her that often enough. Not that she needed a man to tell her that. She had been taking care of herself for a damned long time.

Still, when she left for dinner, she couldn't help looking around the rooftop for evidence that Blaize might have come back some time through the night or today. Finding none, she simply shrugged it off, swallowed the messy cocktail of disappointment and sadness, and rushed down the steps to her car. She made a quick stop at a liquor store on the way to the Bellingers' house and picked out a bottle of dry red that she knew Janie favored.

Dressed in light wash jeans and a long-sleeved bright red t-shirt, she hoped she had nailed a casual, sexy look. She couldn't show up in sweats or yoga pants, though the thought had crossed her mind. She needed to appear strong, put together, and she needed to be strong when she said goodbye, so she'd taken care with her hair and makeup. She needed the look to say *I'm okay. I love you, but I need myself back.*

"Hey." Janie opened the door to her and flashed her a big smile. Konnor eyed the black blouse her friend wore, glad she'd made an effort to look nice. Janie, shorter than Konnor even in her heeled boots, reached for her and pulled her into a tight hug.

"Hi." Konnor hugged her back, caught immediately in the scent of Janie's rich perfume. "Did you have fun last night?"

"We did," Janie answered as she released Konnor and stepped back to let her come inside.

"Where'd you go?" Konnor handed her the bottle of wine.

"Thanks." Janie took her hand and led her into the kitchen. She saw Evan out on the patio, a glass of wine in one hand, and a meat fork in the other. "We went to Sam's," she answered absently. "Had dinner there. And then a few of us went to Sully's for drinks."

"Nice." Konnor nodded.

"Do you want a beer? Or a glass of wine?"

"Um." She settled at the island and told herself she needed to keep a clear head. She should ask for a glass of tea, but that would also set the night down the wrong road. She wanted to stop sleeping with them, not cut herself off from their family and friendship. "How about a beer?"

She watched Janie put the gifted wine on the counter and then grab her a beer from the refrigerator.

"What about you?" Janie handed the bottle to her and waited while Konnor twisted the top off. Because she needed one more second and a shot of confidence-booster to begin, Konnor took a quick sip.

"We were at Buck and Quarter." She shrugged. "I went out and looked at a rental house with him. It was horrible."

"Where's he staying?"

Konnor shrugged and tipped her head when Janie hit her with the hard stare.

"He showed up at my place Thursday again," Konnor told her. "He slept on my couch, but it's not a great place to watch TV, let alone to sleep for eight hours."

"And?"

"I have no idea where he went last night."

"He didn't stay with you?"

"He did not stay with me, Janie," she said quietly. "I have not slept with Blaize Stewart."

"Do you want to?"

Konnor cleared her throat and looked around. "Where are the kids?"

"Change of plans." Janie shrugged. Konnor felt the blood drain from her face when their eyes met. She couldn't hide her discomfort. Janie simply raised her eyebrows. "They're not eating with us, but I'm sure they'll be in and out through the night."

Konnor nodded.

"Evan's grilling steaks," Janie told her.

"Okay."

"I thought you would bring him with you."

"He heard your invite," Konnor mumbled. Janie turned her back to her and started gathering utensils and plates. "He's not interested."

"Not interested?" Janie glanced at her over her shoulder. "Sweetheart, he's definitely interested in you. How could you have missed the tension in your kitchen last Saturday? Evan sensed the way Blaize felt about you the second he saw him."

"Blaize isn't into this…lifestyle. And he doesn't approve of anything I do. And after preaching to me last night, he left, and that's that."

"Nice try." Janie nodded. She waltzed by Konnor to put the utensils and plates on the table.

"What does that mean?"

"Steaks are ready," Evan announced as he stepped inside. Konnor turned quickly to look at him, relieved when he offered her a small, apologetic smile. "Hey. Glad you're here, Konnor."

He set the plate of charbroiled meat on the counter, but when Konnor slid off the barstool and stepped toward him, he gathered her in his arms to hold her.

"I'm sorry." She turned her face to his neck and slipped her arms around his waist.

"You have nothing to be sorry for," he assured her. "Last night was my fault."

She nodded when she pulled away from him, but she ducked her head and turned away. They sat together at the table, the same as they had that first night she had come to apologize for ghosting on them the night of the Wild Canyon party. The same as they had the next morning when they had breakfast after spending the night in bed together.

Konnor was jumpy. Not particularly hungry, but she did her steak justice. But making sure she ate the steak meant not eating much with it. Naturally, Janie noticed. When dinner was over, Konnor stacked the plates, but Janie shook her head and pushed them to the side of the table. Evan poured more wine for himself and Janie and then grabbed a second beer for Konnor.

When he joined them at the table again, Konnor almost asked for whiskey.

"So." Evan took a drink and put his glass down. "Where's he at? Why didn't he come with you?"

8

"**C**an we not make this about him?"

Her words came out as a whisper, but the whisper was loud in the quiet room. Evan and Janie exchanged a look. Konnor ducked her head and rubbed the back of her neck.

"So, there is a *this*? We're here to talk about this?"

"I can't keep doing this." Konnor took a deep breath and winced at the pain it caused. Her throat hurt, but she forced herself to look up, to meet first Janie's eyes and then Evan's.

"And it's not because of him?" Janie asked her.

"Before he showed up last week, I just had this…feeling. That it's time to…"

"Did Janie and I do something? Did I do something to upset you, Kon?"

"No." Konnor glanced at Evan, shook her head, and closed her eyes. She had nowhere to hide, but looking at them was too hard, and neither of them was going to let her walk away.

"The sex is getting stale?"

"Evan, not at all." She swallowed hard. "Look. You guys are married. I know, I know. You've told me a million times you have an unconventional marriage, and that you want me involved like I am."

"Is it because of Cabo?"

Konnor met his eyes, surprised and a little bit irritated with Evan's question.

"No." She groaned and pushed back from the table. "No. And yes. It's about a million little things, and it just all adds up to I can't do this anymore."

"I knew eventually this would happen." Evan shrugged. He didn't sound angry; worse than that, he sounded resigned.

"Look." Konnor drew a deep breath. "I love you guys. I really, truly love you both so much, and that's what you guys can't get. What you can't feel. You have each other—"

"You know we love you," Janie reminded her.

Konnor winced and nodded. "But you guys have *each other*. You guys can walk down the street together, holding hands. You guys can show affection for each other in public. You have a house together. You have children. You have Cabo and the beach and any other damned thing you want because you're married."

"You want to be free," Evan said quietly. "To find the same for yourself."

The knot in her throat was so big, Konnor could only nod.

"Do you want that with him?"

"I don't know," she whispered. "I don't know. I have to do this one thing at a time. I can't sort out how I feel about him when I don't know who I am without you guys. Without... the other stuff."

"Okay." Janie sighed and pushed her hair off her shoulders. "Okay, Kon, we get that."

"I hate this." Konnor pressed her lips together and took a moment to breathe, to find the calm she needed to push through this conversation. "I don't want to lose you guys. I still want to be part of your family."

"You are," Evan said simply.

"You're the first people…" She cleared her throat. "No one's ever…loved me like…well. Just…that. I don't even know what my own parents thought of me, and I grew up okay with that. You don't miss what you don't have, and I thought what I *had* was okay, and then you guys came along, and now…"

"How about this?" Janie nibbled on her lip. "Nothing has to change. Except the obvious. You're always welcome here. With us. At our house."

Konnor nodded. "Thank you."

"He's welcome here," Janie continued. "If he loves you. If he's gonna take care of you, we want to get to know him."

"He can't look at me without knowing…who I am…what I've done." Konnor shrugged. "As much I would like to think we could be together, I don't think it's what he wants."

"I think what Janie means is that we lost sight of you….and your freedom to be and do what you want. And if you find someone to love you, then we hope he lets you stay part of our family."

Konnor nodded. She loved that they'd promised her she would always be part of the family, but she honestly believed she wasn't going to find love as they knew it. Even if she had a fling with Blaize, he would never love her.

"You still don't look happy, Kon." Janie touched the back of her hand. "What's going on in that head of yours?"

She met Janie's eyes and held the look for a long, quiet moment. Finally, she laughed and shook her head. It struck her that she was asking for an out, but that left them together and maybe they would search for someone to take Konnor's place. The thought shattered inside her, making her bleed, and embarrassing her for being so needy.

"Nothing."

"Tell me," Janie insisted.

"I have no right to feel anything." Konnor took a big swallow of her beer. "But I do."

"What do you mean?"

Konnor shifted her gaze to Evan.

"It kills me to think you'll find someone else." It hurt to say the words. "I know Janie's been into this lifestyle a lot more wholeheartedly than you are, Evan. But the thought of not being with you is bad enough. If you find someone else, someone to take my place, I won't be able to take it."

Janie flinched and ducked her head.

"I'm sorry, Janie. God, I'm sorry. I love you, but it hurts so much to think of losing you, Evan."

"Okay." Evan stood up. "Okay. Janie, hon, we've talked about this."

Janie nodded.

"Wait. You've talked about this? About me?"

"I know you're in love with Evan." Janie licked her lips. "I've known that since we've all been together."

Konnor bit her lip.

"Just hard to actually hear you say it."

"You're my friend, Janie. Being in love with your husband. Sleeping with both of you." Konnor shrugged. "This is why I can't keep doing this. I want things from him that I can't have. That I shouldn't want."

"I know," Janie agreed. "I know."

"Do you wanna be with him, Konnor?" Evan asked quietly. She watched him rub Janie's shoulders. Looked away. Fought the ridiculous wave of envy and the equally crazy pull to Blaize.

"He doesn't—"

"Do *you* want to be with *him*?" Evan asked again. "Don't tell me what Blaize wants or doesn't want."

"I wish things were different," Konnor said softly. "I've still got some of that teenage girl in me, because yes, I want to be with him. I want him to love me, and I know he doesn't. I know he can't. And I want you to love me, and I know you do, but not enough and not in the way I need to be loved."

Evan nodded, as if to urge her to keep going.

"Not in the way I…"

"Say it," he commanded her.

"Deserve to be loved," she finished in a whisper.

"Exactly." He trailed his hand over Janie's shoulders and moved around the table to take Konnor in his arms again. She stood without hesitation and pressed into him. Evan held her tight, and though she didn't cry, she wanted to. Because she was pretty sure Blaize didn't see it that way. He had asked her to choose him, and she had just now, but would it ever be enough? Or would he always look at her and see the choices she made before him?

"I love you," she whispered.

"I love you, too," Evan assured her. "And no one's gonna take your place."

"I'm sure you could find another third at Wild Canyon." She shook her head against his chest and reached up to cup his neck with her hand.

"You're not a third," he argued. "You're not with us for thrills. It's not just sex. And you know that."

"I have no right to ask that of you."

Evan shrugged. "I have no interest in replacing you. I'm in love with Janie. I love you. We can take sex out of that equation, Konnor, but it doesn't change the way I feel about you."

Janie stood and pushed her chair back. "So. Whipped cream would definitely be more fun in the bedroom, but I did make dessert."

Konnor felt Evan's laugh rumble up from his belly.

Behind him, Janie was busy cutting what appeared to be apple pie.

"I'm sorry," Evan said quietly. "I swore to myself I wouldn't do this to you. That I wouldn't tie you down. And then I did exactly that."

"You did a lot more than tie me down, Ev," Konnor murmured. "I'm not gonna forget that."

"I know."

He tipped her chin up to kiss her. Konnor expected a quick, sweet goodbye peck, but Evan's kiss was long and soft, and the tenderness brought to mind the way Blaize Stewart had kissed her.

Their first kiss.

She'd crushed on him from the time she had turned thirteen, and finally, at the age of twenty-seven, he'd kissed her for the first time. The fact that she was standing here kissing Evan and thinking about Blaize told her ending this part of her relationship with the Bellingers was the right thing to do.

"Konnor, do you want beer with your pie?" Janie asked skeptically.

"No." Konnor pulled away from Evan and looked at Janie.

"Wine?" Janie offered, but Konnor wasn't a big wine drinker, so Evan was already moving toward the cabinet with the liquor bottles to get her a shot of bourbon.

"I can't drink that and drive," she argued.

"Well, then, you can stay here," Evan suggested. "Believe it or not, we do have a guest room. And there's a lock on the door."

Konnor laughed softly.

"It's okay," Janie promised her. Konnor turned to look at her friend, now standing by her at the table. "That you're in love with him. We let things get pretty complicated."

"I never thought I would love anyone." Konnor cleared

her throat and pushed her hair off her face. "Not sure crushes mean much in the real world."

"They do when they turn into love," Janie told her.

"I think it's too soon to say that, Janie," Konnor argued. "And he left last night without a goodbye."

"So, call him." Evan squeezed close to the table, kissed Janie's shoulder, and reached to set Konnor's drink at her place.

"I can't. I don't have his number. He doesn't have mine." She shrugged again. "I guess we'll see if he shows up again at my place."

"How did he find you without your number?"

Konnor perched on the edge of her chair and watched Janie serve dessert. Evan refilled his and Janie's glasses and joined them at the table again.

Konnor eyed her slice of pie and wondered what the holidays would be like this year. Usually, the holiday season meant cocktail parties and dinner parties and a lot of extra cash flow coming her way from Ryan and Luke. She flicked her gaze up over Janie and Evan and decided she would make this year different. No need to be on her knees for anyone, anymore, if she didn't want to be there. The Bellingers had just welcomed her into their family—again—with no strings attached.

"He said he'd heard from Luke that I was here, but he also said my stepbrothers wouldn't give him my number."

"But he found you," Evan reminded her. "Because he wanted to."

"He's divorced," she confessed. "But he had hoped to find that I was happy."

"You aren't?" Janie tipped her head.

"Happy enough," Konnor mumbled. "But I don't think that's exactly what he was looking for."

"Does his divorce bother you?"

Konnor looked at Evan, surprised by the question. "Why would it bother me? It's over. In the past."

Evan gave her a pointed look and nodded. "Right."

Because she still loved them—that love was a powerful drug to someone who wasn't used to it—she stayed late. Drank too much. Ate a second piece of pie later in the evening. She and Janie curled up on opposite ends of the couch to annihilate their second desserts, and Evan claimed the recliner and the TV remote.

Two movies and too much whiskey later, she and Janie said goodnight, and Evan walked her to their guest room. Gavin had come home, but after a quick catch up session during which Janie and Evan had quizzed him about what he had been doing, he'd ducked down to the basement and then left the house again after nine.

She lost track of time and whether or not Gavin had come back home, and it crossed her mind as she and Evan made their way down the hall to the guest room—thankfully, it was on the opposite end of the hall, as far away from the master bedroom as she could get—that it might be a good thing that she would never be a parent. If a couple fingers of bourbon did her in, she might lose a little kid in a house of her own.

Evan kissed her goodnight. The warm weight of his hands on her hips and the slide of his warm tongue over hers was welcome and oh, so tempting, but after a few moments, Konnor turned her head slightly and tapped his chest with her fingertips. Hell yes, she wanted him. She wanted his hands to slide her clothes off and stroke her in that delicious, intimate way she'd come to love. She wanted his breath on her neck, behind her ear as she slept.

But she wanted to wake up tomorrow and walk out of the Bellingers' house with her head high and her choice carved in stone. If Blaize ever came back, if he ever showed up again, she wanted to offer herself completely and without doubt.

Janie offered to fix breakfast the next morning, but Konnor's stomach shuddered at the thought. She'd been awake since six, head pounding with remnants of the liquor and not enough sleep.

Damned her thoughts about parenting when she'd gone to bed. She'd dreamt about a baby. As dreams go, she couldn't decipher if the baby in her dream was Gavin Bellinger, the baby Blaize and his ex had lost, or hers. But the idea of the baby being hers had left her curled on her side, the spare pillow hugged tight to her belly, and mind spinning crazy dreams about what her future could have been.

Konnor thanked Janie for the offer, thanked Evan for the travel mug of hot, black coffee, and kissed them both on the cheek before walking out. If she had expected Blaize's truck to be parked at the curb in front of her place, she would have been disappointed. She didn't, though. In fact, she didn't believe she would ever see him again, even if he did stick around Rockfield to work on the clinic project. It wasn't a major metropolitan area, but it wasn't small town America, either. There were fifteen or twenty square miles and a good forty-two thousand people around them to offer a buffer.

She climbed the steps and considered calling Luke. Not for work, but for Blaize's number. Dismissed the thought before she ever jammed her key in the lock to open her door. First of all, she wouldn't beg Blaize to come back. What had her teen years been but one big show, just begging for Blaize Stewart's attention? Never mind that she had fun and sort of didn't regret what she'd done. Every time she'd shucked her clothes before she was even twenty years old, she'd done it with the hopes that he would notice her.

And want her.

And claim her.

She hadn't needed Blaize to rescue her, but God, how she had wanted him to claim her.

Second, she wasn't going to call Luke and remind him that she hadn't been showing up at his cocktail parties. That she was avoiding his and Ryan's phone calls. That she had distanced herself from them, their colleagues, their families.

She *would* like to get to know her nephews.

The thought sent a dull ache through her and made her already churning stomach lurch. Her sister-in-law clearly knew about all the things she had done, all the cash she had pocketed the past few years. Konnor had nothing against her, hard to blame her for how she felt considering Konnor was who she was. But it still made her sad. No kids of her own, and she would never have a relationship with her nephews.

Konnor sipped the coffee Evan had made and took some aspirin. She carried her phone and a glass of water to her bedroom, kicked out of the clothes she'd worn to Janie and Evan's the night before, and climbed into bed. No more wallowing. No more regrets. The only way out was forward, and she'd taken the first step. She'd ended the only love relationship she'd ever had, and though she would miss the intimate relationship she'd had with the Bellingers, she was relieved, too, that they understood her need to make the change.

That first step had been huge and exhausting and terrifying, even for a girl who didn't fear much at all. The rest of her life—without the Bellingers and without the connection to Luke and Ryan—was unknown; even the rest of today looked scary as hell. But she would do it. She would be fine, because Konnor Horton took care of herself and always came out on top.

But the exhaustion from the heavy decision, from thinking about what she suddenly had to lose, and the guy in her past—maybe not the one who got away as Evan suggested, because Blaize had never been hers to begin with —showing up unexpected combined with too much bourbon last night was too much to take on at the moment.

She would sleep first. Maybe she would dream. And maybe those dreams would hurt.

But she would survive. She always did.

———

KONNOR DIDN'T JUST SURVIVE. She blossomed. She threw herself wholeheartedly into her classes and the workload they required. Maybe part of her missed last summer and the class with Evan and watching him talking to the rest of the class and remembering the taste of his skin, but she found she enjoyed the literature class she thought she hated. The one she hadn't wanted to take but was required for a four-year degree.

She opened up more at the bank. Got closer to more co-workers. Went out with Pete Frasier, one of the security guards there. He wasn't Evan, and he wasn't Blaize, but he wasn't one of her stepbrothers' colleagues, either, and Konnor found that she liked him. She had no interest in touching him or kissing him. No desire to peek at anything under his fleece pullover or his jeans, but he was fun, and their dinner and drinks night turned into a semi-regular thing. Part of her worried that there might come a time when Pete decided he wanted more than a buddy to discuss college football stats with, but she decided she would worry about that when the time came.

Janie volunteered her to help with a big Halloween party at their house. Konnor was all in, but she was surprised the Bellingers weren't going to be at Wild Canyon Estates for the night. When she asked, Janie simply shrugged, announced that maybe she and Evan would slow down their appearances at the parties, and besides, they wanted to do one last big party at the house while Gavin was home.

Konnor couldn't argue with any of that, but the tidbit about quitting the parties—slowing down on the party attendance—made her belly flutter. She was both relieved that Evan wouldn't be around the parties as often and relieved that maybe Janie and Evan would be happy with the marriage as it was meant to be in the beginning.

She and Janie spent several evenings at the Halloween store, debating over ridiculous decorations that ranged from downright creepy—a zombie child on a swing that gave Konnor the willies—to over-the-top gory—an animated monster holding a severed head. They considered costumes, rolled their eyes over some and laughed at several. Evan had something in mind, but he refused to tell either of them. Janie accused him of planning to be Hugh Hefner one night over cold beers and tacos. Konnor wasn't sure if it was Janie's accusation or Evan's sputtering shock that had her doubled over laughing, but something set her off.

The week before the party, Konnor went out with friends from work, Janie included. Evan met them at Buck and Quarter later in the evening. Konnor waved at him when she saw him walk in, but she stayed at the bar and looked back at Pete. Pete, who it turned out was pining away over Michelle Clooney, the teller who normally worked at Konnor's right side. Konnor was coaching him on what to say to their friend to ask her out.

Pete declared he needed a shot of tequila. Konnor had gone with him to the bar, ready to be his support system, his wingman, his drinking buddy. She didn't love tequila, but she did know that burning need for someone that drove a person to do crazy things to get his or her attention.

She picked her shot up and eyed Pete expectantly.

"This is it, right?" she called over the music which she now knew was much louder near the bar than the booths. She loved the bar, but she hated being here now, after bringing Blaize here. She refused to eat here, hadn't looked at the booth where she and Blaize had sat together weeks ago, and pretended that Blaize Stewart hadn't moved here to Rockfield, temporary or otherwise. Wasn't hard to pretend, she hadn't heard from him or seen him since that last night he'd left her place.

Pete, buzzcut hair and giant, brown eyes, nodded his promise. This was the second night Konnor had done shots with him, hoping he would get his nerve up to ask Michelle out. The first night, she'd spent on the bathroom floor at her place. As much as she wanted to help a friend out, she had no intention of doing that again.

"Promise?" She thumped her fist on Pete's chest and searched his face for sincerity. Well, no, he had sincerity. Apparently, it was the balls he lacked. Konnor was all for feeding him liquid courage, but she wasn't going looking for his balls. She hadn't touched a pair in weeks. She didn't miss it. Not even with Evan, really. There were times when she caught Evan and Janie looking at each other with that love she knew neither of them could ever give her, and she fought off little flashes of envy. But mostly, she was happy with the changes she had made for herself.

"Yes!" Pete yelled and laughed and picked up his shot glass so quickly, Konnor saw the tequila splash and wondered if he would have any to throw back. It amused her to see a grown man so giddy and nervous about asking a woman out, and she loved to tease Pete.

Pete watched her toss her own shot back.

"Go," she ordered him. "Now. Do it." She flattened that fist on his chest, swiped her other hand over her mouth, and tipped her head at Pete. "Dude. Your man card is so on the line right now. I told you she's into you."

She watched Pete gulp a deep breath and nod. Konnor had no idea if Michelle was into Pete or not, but she figured Michelle would let him down easy if she wasn't. She appeared to like him okay, and she was a genuinely nice person, and Pete would never know if he didn't at least ask.

Konnor leaned an elbow on the bar and met Janie's eyes across the room as Pete made his way over to the tall table where Michelle sat with two ladies from the trust department. Janie arched her brows in question, but Konnor only shrugged. If she had to bet, she figured Pete would chicken out yet again.

When the bartender asked if she needed another shot, Konnor swung her gaze around to look at him. She noticed the door on the far side of the room open, saw two guys step inside. There was a table full of rowdy guys near the door. Three of them had their heads tipped to look at the silent TV playing in the corner of the bar. One was looking at his phone. One was watching her.

"Oh God, no," she said with a laugh. She shared a rueful grin with the bartender. "No more tequila. If Pete doesn't ask her out this time, I'm gonna do it for him."

"Yeah? Which one's he after?" The bartender—an older

guy with a gold tooth—rested his palms on the bar and leaned over as if that made it easier to see who Pete was talking to.

"The one with the long braid," Konnor told him. "I spent the night on the bathroom floor the last time we played the tequila game."

"The tequila game."

The voice chased a hard shiver up her spine. Konnor caught her breath, tried to compose herself before turning, and finally looked to her right. Blaize Stewart stood at her side, elbows on the bar.

"You with that guy?" he asked her, nodding over his shoulder in Pete's general direction.

"No." She looked her fill at Blaize's long, unruly blond hair. At the scruff on his cheeks, his chin and over his top lip. At the blue eyes that touched her in ways no man's hands ever could.

"You sure about that?" He narrowed his eyes at her as if he didn't believe her.

"I am absolutely sure about that." She turned back to the bar and asked for a beer.

"Pretty sure I've seen you in here before." Blaize didn't move. "With him. Playing the tequila game."

Konnor's belly flipped at his words, even though he sounded angry. He had seen her here? Was he watching her? Why hadn't he said something to her?

"Well, then, you've seen the girl at the table where he's at, too. Her name's Michelle, and he desperately wants to go out with her."

"And you're, what? Plying him with liquid courage or making a fool of him?"

"How am I making a fool of him?"

Konnor mumbled a thanks to the bartender when he

scooted a longneck bottle toward her. She picked it up and took a long drink before she turned to look at Blaize again.

"Well, apparently, he struck out last time."

"Last time, he never made it close to her table." She rolled her eyes.

"I know the feeling," Blaize said quietly. Konnor snapped her head around to look at him. He didn't explain himself; she didn't ask him to. Instead, she sipped her beer again and stared at him boldly.

"Did you find a place?" she finally asked him. It was something to say, but she found she was interested in his answer. He had vanished from her life again; she was torn between grabbing him with both hands to hold onto him this time and lodging her boot-clad foot in his ass to get him the hell out of her life for good.

He shrugged and nodded. "I did."

"Oh, God." She covered her mouth when the harsh laugh bubbled up from deep inside. "You didn't rent that place we went to, did you?"

His slow grin was like cocaine. Just a glimpse, and she craved more. She ached to touch him, just to brush her fingers over the back of his hand.

"No." He shrugged his eyebrows and held up a finger in the bartender's direction. Konnor watched the older man dig in his cooler until he produced a longneck for Blaize. He wasn't drinking the same thing she was, but the guy at the bar knew what he wanted. Apparently, Blaize came here often. She shifted her eyes to look at the table where she'd spotted him a few minutes ago. Just a few guys, so maybe he hadn't come here with someone, with a woman, but that didn't mean he was still single, either.

He was watching her, waiting for her to meet his eyes when she looked back at him. The last night they were together wedged between them at the bar; Konnor couldn't have stepped closer to him if she wanted to. Blaize wore her past like a shield of protection. A wave of regret so strong it nearly knocked her off her feet rolled over her. To hide from Blaize, and maybe to remind herself that she had moved on, Konnor took a peek at Pete, happy to see that he was at least sitting at the table next to Michelle. She relaxed against the bar as she watched the two of them talk.

"You're really just the wingman, huh?" Blaize twisted around to stare at Pete and Michelle. "Not interested in him?"

"Stop it!" she hissed and thumped his arm to make him turn back to the bar. "Don't stare at him. Good grief, I spent the last night we did shots on my bathroom floor. I don't think I've been that drunk in years."

Blaize tipped his beer up and swallowed more, but he watched her from the corner of his eye.

"Are you here with them?"

"I work with them," she answered, but when she flicked her gaze from Pete and Michelle back to Blaize, she realized he meant Janie and Evan. When she didn't answer, Blaize raised an eyebrow as if to coerce a confession from her.

"No." She shook her head and drained her bottle. "I came with Pete, actually."

"Pete."

"The guy searching for his balls in a tequila bottle," she reminded him. When Blaize narrowed his eyes at her, she rolled hers. "We're friends, Blaize."

"So, you're doing shots with the guy who drove you here?" He turned sideways and dragged his gaze down over her shoulders and her breasts and her hips. To her toes. "Those don't look like good walking shoes."

"I'll manage," she said vaguely. Impatient when his eyes climbed slowly back over her body and lingered on her breasts, Konnor hooked his chin in her hand and forced him to look up. "My eyes are up here, Mr. Stewart."

He studied her silently for a long moment. Konnor's belly twisted in knots, but she knew how to lie and she looked right back at him, fierce and unforgiving.

When he spoke, his words were a shock.

"Wanna dance?"

Konnor drew back in surprise and then looked around. She noticed Janie watching her from the end of the long table where most of the bank employees were sitting. Konnor didn't meet her eyes. True, they were friends now. The best of friends. But they were lovers once, and that sort of intimacy felt wrong right now. With Blaize standing here asking her to dance.

"Here?"

Blaize made a show of looking over his shoulder at seven or eight couples dancing on what was definitely a dance floor. The kitchen had closed at nine, but the bar was packed, and Konnor was aware that there were usually a lot of people dancing. But she'd never been one of those people; in fact, she wasn't much into dancing at all.

Missing homecoming that time when Blaize was a sophomore and he thought she was too young to go. Blowing her stepbrother. Playing party girl. She'd never worn a formal gown, never gone to a single high school dance.

"Is that not a dance floor?" Blaize looked back at her.

"I'm not much of a dancer," she told him.

"I'm not either, but it seems like a damned good excuse to put my arms around you right about now."

Konnor's mouth went dry when he set his bottle down and reached for her hand. She tried to swallow anyway, rubbed her hands over her jeans—funny that she could be nervous about dancing to eighties country music when she was damned near thirty when she had thought dancing was stupid when she was a teenager—and slipped her hand in his. She refused to look at Janie, but her friend patted her butt as they walked by her. Konnor snorted, but she only shook her head when Blaize turned to her and slipped his arms around her waist.

"You went to high school dances," she reminded him. She had to press her lips close to his ear to make herself heard. "And I bet you danced with your wife at your reception."

"I did." He flattened his palms on her back and tugged her in closer. "Doesn't mean I'm good at it, but this was the only excuse I could come up with to put my arms around you right now."

Konnor had no idea who was singing at the moment, but she was glad for the slow, easy beat. All she had to do was stand in Blaize's arms and sway back and forth. She worried what would happen when the music changed. She worried about who Blaize might be here with. She wondered if Evan was watching them and prayed that he wasn't. Wondered if she should wish Evan and Janie weren't here or if that meant she wasn't ready to commit to anything with Blaize. If he asked.

She reminded herself he wasn't going to ask. The fact that he happened to be at this bar on this night at the same time she was meant nothing. She'd brought him here once; it appeared that he had come out tonight with buddies. He saw her doing shots with some guy and assumed the worst—how could she blame him?—and he came over to talk to her.

And now they were dancing. End of story.

Before tonight she had hated dancing, much the same way she'd sworn she wouldn't, couldn't enjoy sex. She hadn't needed that part of the equation before Evan Bellinger made love to her. Standing so close to Blaize, in his arms, was safe and comforting, and she decided she could dance the night away, after all.

Blaize held her tight, her middle pressed snug against his. The rub of his hard cock against her stomach was a slow, careful fire in her inner thighs. Her belly clenched at the thought of that same erection moving inside her and Blaize's hands on her skin. But when he nuzzled her neck with his lips, she wondered about dancing. Maybe it *wasn't* safe.

"Jesus, Blaize," she hissed when he nipped at the skin of her neck with his teeth. Her heartbeat quickened, and she imagined Blaize felt the blood rush through her veins. She felt as safe with him now as if he was a vampire about to take a bite out of her.

"Come with me."

He had said those words to her before, on that last night they'd been together. He had asked her to go look at the rental with him. Bought her dinner. Told her maybe his feelings for her were part of the reason why his side of his marriage had been doomed.

Konnor had been afraid of him. Of what could happen between them.

Now she was afraid of saying no. Of watching him walk away and losing him forever this time.

When he drew back just enough to look her in the eye, she nodded, her cheek pressed to his. The rub of his scruff over her skin sent a flash of heat through her. Before she knew she was moving, she smoothed her fingers over his face and closed her eyes. His kiss was too slow, too tame. That slow, careful fire was climbing, the flames licking her center. Afraid she would burn here in front of everyone, she turned her head slightly and ducked her chin.

"K?"

"Not here, Blaize," she whispered.

She'd grown out of the need for an audience years ago, but now, the only boy, the only man, she'd wanted to notice her was kissing her, and she had no desire to make a show of what she felt for him.

"Do you need to tell your friend? That you're leaving?"

Konnor winced, the dig taking a chunk out of her heart.

"The guy you came here with," Blaize reminded her. Eyes on his, she nodded, but she was reluctant to step away from him. What if the spell was broken when they stepped outside?

Blaize waited patiently for her to move. His fingers linked around her wrists, he simply traced his thumbs back and forth over her skin, letting her make the final decision. Their eyes locked, Konnor hoped she looked fearless. Inside, she shook with the fear that Blaize Stewart would fuck her and forget her.

She swallowed hard and glanced at Pete, who was head to head with Michelle, obviously deep in conversation. Loathe to butt in now, and not certain Pete had any business driving home anyway, Konnor turned her head just as Janie looked up. Evan was talking to Frank Jackson up by the bar.

Janie arched her eyebrows and tipped her head. Konnor answered with a tiny nod.

"Go." Janie nodded.

The quiet outside the bar hit her first. Blaize wrapped himself around her before the October chill could reach her. Arms around her, he cupped her ass in his hands and held on. Breathless with desire, Konnor studied his face, attempting to memorize the desperate need, so she would have it later when he left her.

When he lowered his head to hers, she kissed him. One soft, tender kiss and then Konnor hooked her hands around his neck and pushed her thumbs up into his hair and met his tongue thrust for thrust.

"You're so fuckin' gorgeous," he panted when he turned his head to kiss her cheek and her chin and then her neck. "You have no idea how beautiful you are."

"Blaize." She whimpered when he backed her up against the wall. Just outside the main entrance to the bar, Konnor lifted her right leg and wrapped it around his waist. "Take me home. Please? I want this so much, but not here."

"I know." He nodded, but his lips sought hers and demanded more again. Konnor held on, her fingers tangled in his hair. She kissed him back, eager to please him, to give him what he wanted. She squeezed her leg tighter around him, rubbing her center against his cock, desperate to feel him inside her.

"Please take me home," she whispered. "Make this just me and you. Please, Blaize?" She nipped at his earlobe and gasped in surprise when he pulled away from her. She stared at him silently, waiting for him to argue. To push for her to fuck him here. In front of the bar. To get down on her knees and suck him off, the way she had done so, so many times in the past with their mutual friends.

Or would he walk away again? Leave her desperate to be with him, to feel his love, again?

"Are you drunk?" His voice was hard, unforgiving.

Konnor rested her head on the wall and closed her eyes. To her horror, tears of frustration spilled.

"No."

"Konnor. Look at me."

She shuddered a long, deep breath and finally opened her eyes to look at him.

"If you get in my truck with me right now, there's no going back."

"Please." She nodded.

"I watched you throw back two shots of tequila," he reminded her. "And the last time we saw each other, you were adamant that—"

"I'm not drunk, Blaize." Her voice was thick with need. "I'm not drunk. I'm just the girl who's wanted to be with you this way since she was a kid."

"I don't want to be another regret."

"You're already my biggest regret." She cupped his cheek in her hand and pressed her lips together. "I just wanted you to love me. It's why I've done the things I've done."

"Konnor."

"I wanted your attention," she continued, her voice small

and quiet but sincere, "and when I didn't get it, I needed something…"

"To hurt me?" He tipped his head.

She frowned and dashed at her eyes. "I never did it to hurt you. I was empty inside. And every time I used sex to put a piece of myself back together, I broke a little bit more."

Blaize groaned and yanked her back from the wall into his arms. Konnor threw her arms around him, the hunger replaced now with desperation of a different kind. She didn't need sex so much as she needed Blaize Stewart to love her.

"Make love to me, Blaize."

He nodded and took her hand and nearly dragged her over the parking lot to his truck. She climbed in the driver's side when he unlocked the door, banged her knees on the steering wheel, and scooted over to give him room. Inside the cab, the October chill finally caught up with her, and her teeth chattered with cold and nerves. Blaize started the truck and glanced at her.

"Your place is closer than mine," he told her.

"Okay."

"Have you…"

Sitting so close her thigh rubbed his, she twisted a bit to look at him. But there wasn't much light in the cab of the truck, and she didn't want him to turn the dome light on.

"No one's been at my place since you left the last time," she assured him.

He threw his head back and blew out a long, hard sigh. Konnor nibbled on her lip, scared that he would change his mind. That he would tell her no. That he had been dicking with her from the beginning and had no intention of touching her.

"You guys do it at their house? Don't they have kids?"

Konnor flinched and turned back square in the seat. She reminded herself that she had made the choices that led to this very moment, including the choices that inspired Blaize's worry, his questions. His distrust.

"You asked me to choose," she whispered. "I made my choice, Blaize. The night you walked out, I made my choice."

"You haven't—"

"No."

"You didn't call me."

"I don't have your number," she reminded him.

"We wasted all that time?"

"No." She shook her head. "That time alone for me?" She swallowed hard, still afraid to look at him. "It's been good. I'm good, Blaize. I needed that time to get my head on straight."

"But you're sure? About us?"

"Are you gonna fuck me?" She leaned back and rolled her head on the seat to look at him. "Or is there more?"

"I thought about you a lot. In school." He took her hand. "When I was away at school. When I was kissing other girls."

Green with jealousy over the thought of Blaize with other girls, with his wife, Konnor turned her head away and stared out the windshield.

"I don't wanna know about you kissing other girls."

"Really?" He leaned into her and rested his chin on her head. "I watched my friends fuck you, and you don't wanna know about me kissing other girls?"

"I can't stand the thought of you with anyone else."

"And I hated knowing what you were doing with everyone but me."

"Blaize—"

"We've said this before. My point is—and I said this before, too—I thought about you when I was with my wife. And when Kristi and I divorced, I waited…until the sting of failure, the grief, before what I felt for her was gone…and then I came looking for you."

Konnor nodded. "But what are you looking for with me, Blaize? One night?"

"The Konnor Horton I know would jump out of this truck if I told her what I want."

"Maybe that's changed," she whispered.

"Right now, I want you flat on your back, and I wanna be balls deep inside you. And I wanna hear you panting and moaning and screaming my name."

"I want that, too."

Blaize tipped her head back to kiss her. Konnor caught his hand when he dropped it at her waist to fiddle with her button.

"I'm too tall to get flat on my back in your truck," she argued. "And I don't want an audience when I'm with you, Blaize."

———

THE DRIVE WAS the longest four minutes of her life. Blaize had soft rock playing on the radio, and John Mayer sere-naded them. The song was slow and sexy, which didn't help the sexual tension in the air. It wasn't late when he parked in front of her apartment, but the streets were dead, and only a few houses were lit with lamplight. When Blaize cut the engine and reached for the keys, Konnor unbuckled her seat-belt and turned to him. Torn between needing to be inside, alone with him, and needing to touch him, to feel the warmth of his skin, the beat of his heart under her hand, she turned sideways in her seat and reached for him.

She still expected him to pull away, but he leaned in when she cupped the back of his neck and tugged his face closer to hers. His skin was hot on her hand, and she squeezed his neck gently as she kissed him. Before Evan and Janie, Konnor hated kissing. Something about being mouth to mouth with someone, about opening her eyes and finding someone so close, possibly watching her, made her uncomfortable. So much easier to keep things sexual and impersonal, though some people didn't seem to get the difference.

Kissing Evan and Janie had been a lesson in sensuality. A lesson in love. In intimacy. The thought of Evan's mouth over hers, his tongue stroking hers was so much more thrilling than putting her mouth on his cock or feeling his mouth between her legs. Maybe her life was supposed to happen just as it had, because without the Bellingers, Konnor might have skipped these sweet, intimate kisses she craved now with Blaize.

He moved, and Konnor's low moan of appreciation was muffled by his lips on hers. He slid his hand over her waist, his fingers stroking the bare skin between her jeans and the tank she wore under her denim jacket. Stunned by the jolt of electricity there under his fingertips, Konnor broke the kiss and turned her head slightly.

"What?" Blaize pressed his lips to her forehead. "What's wrong?"

"I don't wanna wait."

"We're almost there," he reminded her.

"I know." She nodded. A little bit breathless, she turned her face and latched onto his lips again. "I've been thinking about this for years, Blaize. I can't wait another second."

Rather than argue with her, he stroked her skin again and this time, he slid his fingers into the front of her jeans. The backs of his knuckles brushed low over her belly.

"Let's go inside," he whispered.

She shook her head. "I can't walk right now. Your hand there is making me weak in the knees."

"All those times you were…" He let his words trail off. Konnor rested her forehead on his chin and nodded. "I never heard you come. When I watched porn, the girls were always screaming and writhing like they were dying with pleasure."

"You watched porn?"

He nodded, his head still pressed to her forehead.

"But you wouldn't watch me? You wouldn't look at me?"

"I looked, Konnor, and I wanted to be with you." He kissed her head again. "But I wanted it to be just you and me somewhere."

"Because you were embarrassed." She moved her hand then, trailed her fingers over the fly of his jeans.

"Well, yeah, but because I wanted more for you."

She swallowed hard.

"I would go home after you were doing that stuff, and watch porn and jack off. Thinking about you."

"I didn't know." Her whisper was gruff with pain, sadness. "I thought you hated me."

"I hated what you let them do to you," he corrected her.

"Blaize." She worked the button of his jeans and slowly tugged his zipper down. "I need this."

"Let's go inside," he urged her.

"Now. I need you inside me right now."

Blaize caught her hand as she felt the heat of his erection on the back of her knuckles.

"Commando?" She laughed softly. "Really?"

"Yep."

"Always?"

"Yep."

"Ohmygod." She kissed him again. "You weren't wearing underwear that morning in my kitchen? When you fixed me breakfast?"

"Nope."

"You had those sexy shorts on—"

"And I had serious wood for you. I thought I was gonna die when you were checking me out."

"Please let me touch you." She circled her thumb over the crown of his cock.

He kissed her again, his lips and his tongue demanding and harsh, and still, Konnor met his thrusts with her own hunger, her own need.

"I want to undress you and lay you down." He kissed a trail over her cheek and then nipped at her earlobe. "Lick you all over. I wanna sink my teeth into you and mark you as mine."

Konnor curled her fingers around his steel shaft and squeezed him gently.

"Okay. But we could do it here first." She scooted closer to him and turned her face just enough to capture his lips in another kiss.

"I wanna make you come, Konnor."

"Okay," she whispered against his chin and his neck. She nibbled on his skin and stroked his cock again. "But I'm not a screamer."

Blaize covered her hand on his cock with his own to still her movements.

"I wanna know what sound you make when you come." He spoke with a sincerity so fierce and raw, Konnor felt his words like a caress. "I wanna watch your face. I wanna see your body tense and then watch your face when you fall."

She drew her hand away from him and leaned back just enough to unbutton her own jeans.

"Is this a good idea?" His voice was gruff.

Konnor's heart pounded painfully hard, and her fingers turned to ice. She looked up at him, certain he had changed his mind.

"Blaize," she sobbed.

"I meant out here," he told her. "In the truck."

"We can be quick," she promised him.

"I don't want quick, K," he argued. But she eased her jeans

down over her hips, drawing his gaze. "Can you—? Like this?"

She kicked off one heeled boot and then wiggled that leg from her jeans.

"We could have been inside by now." He grinned when she met his eyes.

"If we do it here." She skimmed her fingers over his cock again. "Can you do it again inside?"

"Are you asking me if I can get it up twice?"

Konnor arched her eyebrows, but the street was dark, and the interior of his truck was darker.

"Maybe," she mumbled in case he couldn't see her face clearly.

"I've had a hard-on for you for years, Konnor Horton," he told her. "I could fuck you from now 'til next Tuesday and not get enough."

"Blaize." She scooted closer to him and eased her leg over him to straddle him. "What if I need more than next Tuesday?"

"Fuck." He groaned when she lowered herself to rub her clit over the tip of his cock.

"Oh, Blaize." She wound her arms around his neck when he lifted his hips from the seat.

"Condom," he mumbled as he tugged his wallet from his pocket.

"Remember that night I took my shirt off in front of you? When I was changing my clothes?"

"Like I could forget it?"

"Why didn't you touch me?" She pressed her cheek to his and then flicked her tongue over the shell of his ear.

"I told you I don't share."

In the darkness, Konnor heard him open the condom. She rested her knees on the seat at his sides and pressed her forehead to his to watch him roll the condom on.

"I wish I could see you better."

He laughed softly. "You insisted we do this here," he reminded her.

"Oh my God." She groaned out loud when Blaize curled his fingers around her hips and eased her down over his cock. Konnor shifted over him to take him as deep as she could. "You feel so good, Blaize."

"I didn't want you to have to do the work." He leaned forward and latched his open mouth on her neck. "I want to make you crazy, K. I wanna make you beg for more."

"Blaize." She cupped his chin in her hand and tipped his face up. "Kiss me."

This kiss, with his cock buried inside her, was wet and hot, and Konnor moved over him, riding him with a slow, easy rhythm. Blaize cupped her ass cheeks in his hands, urging her to move faster.

"Fuck, Konnor, you feel so fuckin' good on me."

With her lips parted, hovering near his, she worked her hips, clenched his cock with her pussy, and eased him in and out, faster and harder, until his body seized, and his shoulders tensed. Blaize lifted his ass from the seat again, hands on her hips to hold her down on his cock, as his orgasm ripped through him. Konnor licked his lips then, her tongue searching for his, for that intimate touch Evan had taught her to crave.

Blaize kissed her, but he was breathless, and he sank back to rest against the seat.

"Incredible," he told her.

She moved with him, kissing the corner of his mouth, and then licking a trail over the scruff on his face, his chin, to his neck.

"Too fast." His voice was gruff. "Way too fast."

"Come up with me." She pressed the words to his neck

and then pulled his shirt collar open far enough to rake her teeth over his collar bone.

"In a minute."

"Blaize."

"I want my mouth here." He moved his hands over her hips again. Fingers wide over her, he spread her open with his thumbs. She shivered, though she was still mostly clothed.

"I don't think we can manage that here," she said with a grin.

"No, but we've got room for this," he told her as he pressed his thumb to her clit.

"We could go upstairs first."

"Nope." He rubbed the nub of sensitive skin in big, slow circles. "I won't walk away from you without this."

"I'm not asking you to walk away—"

"Not even for two minutes." He shook his head. "Show me who you are, K. Let me see you come."

Konnor licked her lips, worried that she wouldn't come in their current position. Blaize worked her clit with steady, even strokes, and the telltale warmth of orgasm teased and faded.

"You can't see me," she whispered.

"I can see your eyes."

"What if the neighbors see us?" She ducked her head and shifted slightly over him, shivering again when he moved his hand to stroke her where their bodies met.

Blaize's sharp laugh rang out in the cab of the truck.

"Now you're worried about the neighbors seeing us?"

"I'm not gonna come like this," she argued. "Not out here. Like this."

"No?" He pinched her clit between his thumbs and made her moan softly.

"I don't think I can."

"What if I were licking you there?" He offered her a lazy grin. "Would that do it?"

"Mm." She felt her cheeks go warm. "It would help."

"And if I sucked on you? Here?" He dragged the pad of his thumb over her clit. "Would that feel good?"

"Would you do that?"

"I will suck on every inch of your body when we go upstairs."

"Blaize." She whimpered as he continued to stroke her. "Let's just go—"

"What if I did this?" He cupped one breast in his hand and brushed her nipple through her tank and her silk bra.

"Feels good," she gushed.

"And this?" He lifted his head from the seat and bent her back a bit over the steering wheel. Konnor gasped and moaned and called his name when he closed his teeth over her tank and her bra and her nipple.

"Will you still suck on every inch of my body?" she whispered hopefully.

"Put your pant leg back on," he said with a chuckle. "I'll race you to your bed."

"I have a perfectly good table we could use. Some great wall space—"

"Nope." He kissed her again, his lips hot and wet on hers. The wet spot he left on her tank and bra stuck to her nipple. "We're going straight to your bed for rounds two through five."

"Five?" she whispered.

"Orgasms two through five," he clarified.

"You can go five times?"

"I'm good for three," he promised her. "But I can and will deliver you until you beg for mercy."

"You're gonna give me five orgasms? Five more? Or does this one count?"

"Five more."

"Blaize?"

"Hmm?"

"What about tomorrow?"

"We start over. I'm good for another five before we have breakfast."

She laughed softly. "And your wife said you were better in the kitchen than the bedroom?"

"K?" He kissed her cheek. "Imagine what I can do with chocolate covered strawberries. Or a can of cake frosting."

Konnor blinked in the darkness.

"Did you mean it?" She captured his hands and held them still.

"Mean what?"

"When you said I might be your reason for not being able to make things work with your wife?"

"Hard to make my wife happy when I was always in love with you."

Konnor sighed and lifted his fingers to her lips. "It was always you."

"Konnor."

"I'm so sorry." She rolled her lips inward and ducked her head. "I wish I could undo all of it and just have you."

"Maybe this is just exactly the way it was supposed to happen." He freed his hands and slipped his arms around her. "Maybe if we would have messed around and dated when we were kids, we would have burned out fast and gone our separate ways."

"Maybe." She nodded.

"I hated all the others, the years between us. But it's okay, if this is it. If this is how it works out. You and me together."

"Blaize?"

"Let's go." He nodded.

They scooted away from each other, Konnor slipping

back to her side of the truck cab. She tugged her pant leg on as Blaize tucked his cock back in his jeans and carefully zipped and buttoned up. They climbed from the truck, Konnor carried her shoes in her right hand, the fingers of her left entwined with his as she led him up the steps to her apartment.

SNEAK PEEK BLOW ME A KISS

Bronson Hart flashed a grin—women had swooned at his grin for years, and he knew it—as he twisted the top off a longneck and set the bottle on the makeshift bar. From the corner of his eye, he saw the guy claim the beer and lift it to his mouth, but Bronson kept his focus on the lady. Petite and athletic. Hooded gray eyes and plump, kissable-looking lips.

"Decide?" He arched his eyebrows now as he waited for her to answer. Her soft laughter was thick and warm, and when she tipped her head back, her riotous dark curls flowed around her head. "No hurry."

There wasn't any hurry. Bronson had all night. He could stand here and watch this woman—he hadn't met her before —study the row of craft beer bottles and consider every mixed drink known all night if it took her that long to make a decision. And if he got bored looking at her—he wouldn't; Bronson hadn't met a woman yet who bored him—all he needed to do for entertainment was look around.

Wasn't much to see yet, but within the hour the party would be in full swing, Frank and Donna Jackson's house would be packed, and Bronson would have his pick of women to watch. Not that he needed to see skin to find a woman attractive. But if the women here wanted to strut around in various states of undress, Bronson was going to enjoy the view.

The woman at the bar asked for a glass of pinot. Bronson considered suggesting she start with something a bit stronger. He often made that suggestion to the women, simply because most of them had no idea what sort of party they were attending, and the liquor curbed the anxiety. He poured the pinot without comment, though, since she was here with a date. Maybe being at a Wild Canyon Estates party as part of a couple was a little less daunting than showing up single.

Donna Jackson approached the bar, but she was looking around the open living area. Bronson wished the couple a fun night and turned his attention to Donna. He used to work with her at the bank. And he'd fingered her out back by the pool at one of the first parties. Fucked her a time or two back in the old days, before he'd given up the parties. Their friendship stayed intact; Bronson had no judgment about the activities or the guests who partook in said activities. He'd simply withdrawn from everything after getting the shit stomped and kicked out of his heart. Donna fussed over him at work after the big breakup, and she continued to text him occasionally when he left the bank and went all in with an old college buddy on a startup bar and restaurant. She had said she missed him so often that Bronson thought she was flirting, hinting that she wanted to mess around with him again. Instead, she told him that she and her husband Frank wanted to hire him as their party bartender.

He'd fought it for a week or two, long enough that Donna upped the payment offer so high he couldn't refuse. Not to mention that view. Bronson saw more tits in one night than a frat party did in a weekend. Lot more than that, too. Who needed porn flicks when he could stand behind a bar, sip on good bourbon or a cold beer, and watch real women—short, tall, thin, curvy, black, white—go down on guys, on each other, ride somebody and shake the walls with their orgasms, and then pick up a pay check at the end of the night and go home and wait for next time?

Okay, honestly, there were times he would rather have his own woman. Tucked away in his bed, in his house, all to himself. But it wasn't going to happen, and Bronson had accepted that. Love, kids, blah blah blah—not in the cards for him. He had game, he had that charming smile, and he had—according to several women, Donna included—all the right moves. So, sex wasn't a problem. He could have had his choice of women with the snap of his fingers, but he wasn't that guy. He loved the whole game. The flirting and the conversation and the teasing and the sweet, soft kisses that led to slow, wet kisses that led to roaming hands—

Exactly why he'd had his heart shredded and then swept up in a pile and handed back to him.

Still, he played a little bit at the parties. Not as much as he used to. Mostly, he was okay with watching it all from behind the bar.

"Do you need a drink?" Bronson shuffled down to the end of the bar and leaned over to rest his elbows. "Maybe a shot of Bronson?"

"Is that on the menu?" Donna asked hopefully.

Bronson chuckled.

"Don't tease me." She frowned at him. "It's been a long day."

"So, it sounds like you do need a shot of something stiff."

Donna's laughter rang loud and happy.

"Just a beer."

No surprise. Neither of the Jacksons drank much on a party night. They ran a tight ship, both of them always observing their guests, making sure everyone had a good time but also ensuring everyone's safety.

Bronson stepped away from her and selected a longneck bottle from the cooler. He twisted the top off, but he didn't relinquish the beer when he stepped closer to her. Donna saw him leaning her way, so she stretched over the bar to meet him halfway. Their lips met in a quick but intimate kiss.

"Maybe you and Frank need to take center stage tonight," he suggested as he had several times before. The hosts did, on occasion, get down and dirty for the rest of them, acting out sexy scenes in the middle of the room. Donna had been married to Frank for as long as Bronson had known her. She loved the guy to the moon and back. But they had opened their marriage to experimentation a few years ago, and then they'd opened their home for others who wanted a safe place to play and experiment with new things and new people. The woman was full-throttle sexy; so much so that Bronson didn't mind looking at Frank's buff shoulders and back and perfect ass or his giant cock when he was doing Donna. Watching the pleasure build in her face, watching her body coil, ready to explode—hearing her scream Frank's name when she came—worth it to Bronson.

"You ready for this?" Donna asked him when she pulled away.

Bronson grinned and took a drink of her beer before handing it over to her.

"You bet I am."

Eyes locked with his, she tipped the bottle up for a drink.

"Do you ever wish things were different?"

ABOUT THE AUTHOR

TE Sheridan is the author of thirty women's fiction and contemporary romance novels. She lives in the Midwest with her husband and two children.

ALSO BY TE SHERIDAN

www.ingramcontent.com/pod-product-compliance
Lightning Source LLC
Chambersburg PA
CBHW030541130626
46552CB00006B/2364